THE TRIAL OF
ST. JOHN

Also by David J. Diamond

A Bucket of Whitewash

THE CHINESE PUZZLE
From Friend to Foe
How did it happen?

THE TRIAL OF ST. JOHN

Was the Gospel of John Responsible for the Holocaust? You Decide.

DAVID J. DIAMOND

ARCHWAY
PUBLISHING

Archway Publishing books may be ordered through booksellers or by contacting:

Archway Publishing
1663 Liberty Drive
Bloomington, IN 47403
www.archwaypublishing.com
1 (888) 242-5904

ISBN: 978-1-4808-7311-7 (sc)
ISBN: 978-1-4808-7312-4 (e)

Library of Congress Control Number: 2018914718

Print information available on the last page.

Archway Publishing rev. date: 01/30/2019

"The Jews are the odious assassins of Christ, and for killing God there is no expiation possible. ….Christians may never cease vengeance, and the Jews must live in servitude forever. God always hated the Jews, and whoever has intercourse with Jews will be rejected on Judgment Day. It is incumbent upon all Christians to hate the Jews."

— Saint John Chrysostom
Patriarch of Constantinople, Fourth Century

"…Auschwitz would not have been possible without Christianity."

— Elie Wiesel
From: Harry James Cargas in *Conversations with Elie Wiesel* (page 34)

Dedication

THIS BOOK IS DEDICATED with love and admiration to my wife Jeanne who has been my dear companion on life's long journey.

Jeanne sang many roles with the Lyric Opera of Chicago.

She is also a Cantorial Soloist whose beautiful voice has inspired so many.

Jeanne is the devoted and proud mother of our children: Mark, Larry and Debbie and grandmother to our six wonderful grandchildren.

Thank you Jeanne for your encouragement in bringing this book to the public and for your many helpful suggestions.

Acknowledgement

My sincere thanks to my son Mark for his dedicated editing of the manuscript for *The Trial of St. John.*

My thanks also to my other son Larry for enlightening me about the mysteries of the computer world. Larry also read the manuscript and made important suggestions.

I am also grateful to my lifelong friend Dr. Mitzie Eisen for her enthusiasm after reading the manuscript and urging me to publish this book.

My thanks also to my sister Shiphra Davis for her valuable suggestions and to my family and friends who took the time to read the manuscript and share their ideas with me: Marilyn Reinish, Ellen Lees, James Lees, Leonard and Phyllis Kipnis.

Introduction

ANTI-SEMITISM PLANTED THE SEEDS for the Holocaust. Where did hatred for the Jews come from? Who started it?

This story begins with the brutal sexual assault of a twelve year-old Jewish girl by a gang of boys. Her father, a history professor, wanted to know why those boys hated Jews. His research led him to the New Testament and the Gospel of John.

Woven into an exciting story with memorable characters is a fictional *Trial of St. John*. John defends his Gospel as do other key figures in the intriguing plot.

Is the Gospel of John responsible for the Holocaust? Both sides of the argument are fairly presented. You decide.

Chapter

One

THE FOUR YOUNG MEN drinking Coors in the White Hen store parking lot watched the girl get off the Metra train.

"Dumb kid should know not to go through the park at night," Luke said as he watched her cross the dark expanse of grass that stretched along the railroad tracks.

"Hey man, this is Highland Park, not Chicago. Everyone cuts across the park," John replied taking another gulp of his beer. The two other boys murmured agreement.

"Well, I think it is our civic duty to protect the young lady from any evil characters who may be lurking around," Luke persisted.

"No one is around," John said before taking a swig of beer.

"I know that dummy. You want to just sit around and get stoned all night, or do you want to have some fun?"

"Doing what Luke?" John asked.

"Let's offer the little Jew girl a ride home," Luke laughed.

"How do you know she's Jewish?" Matt in the back seat chimed in.

"All the girls are Jewish out here. It's Jew Town. I bet she's just another spoiled little Jewish princess," Luke replied after another swallow of beer.

"I bet she's not," Pete said.

"How much you want to bet?" Luke challenged him.

"Another six-pack," Pete replied.

"OK. Let's go ask her." Luke took another swig of beer and started up the red Toyota.

Jenny Sanders looked behind her. No one was there. She felt a little funny, a little scared. She walked faster. Her Dad had dropped her off at Gloria's around dinner time. She and Gloria were going to rehearse a skit for the temple youth group. The plan was for Jenny to sleep over so the girls could gossip all night.

Unfortunately, Gloria got sick after dinner. Gloria's father offered to drive Jenny home, but Jenny insisted on taking the train from Winnetka. Her house was only a few blocks from the train station and it was only 7 p.m. What could go wrong in Highland Park?

Now she was sorry she had not accepted the ride home. Her folks would be peeved at her for not calling. They were out for a rare dinner date with friends and Jenny did not want to disturb them. The park was dark. No heavenly lights pierced the cloudy sky. A gentle wind caressed her delicate features and her long black hair fluttered in the breeze.

Jenny saw a red Toyota pull up to the curb near the tennis courts where she was headed. From the light of the street lamp she could see a car full of boys. Jenny decided not to take any chances. She turned around and started running to the White Hen store. It was a block away, but she was a fast runner. Jenny looked behind her. Two boys were chasing her. Jenny dropped her overnight bag and raced for safety. She didn't make it.

Luke drove the Toyota across the grass. Suddenly, the car was right in front of her. Jenny couldn't stop in time and crashed against the fender. She crumbled to the ground. Two boys picked her up and pushed her into the back seat. The Toyota sped out of the park and stopped across the street from the White Hen.

Luke whispered instructions to Pete. Pete went into the store and came back in a few minutes with a six-pack of Coors and a brown paper bag. The car drove off with Jenny squeezed in the back seat between two husky boys. She was a little bruised, but not badly hurt.

"You guys are going to get in a lot of trouble if you don't let me out of here right now," Jenny demanded.

"First we have to settle a bet," Luke said calmly. "See, I said you were Jewish, and Pete bet me you were not. So who's right?"

"I'm Jewish. So what's the big deal? Are you some kind of Nazi freak?"

"Oh no way. We're 100 percent Americans," Luke replied.

"OK. So you won your bet. Now let me out of here!"

"I guess you don't know what night this is," Luke said.

"It's Friday night. So what?" Jenny struggled to stay calm, but her heart was pounding with fear.

"See? That's the trouble with you Jews," Luke continued in a teasing voice. "You don't care about other people. Tonight is not just any Friday night. It's special. Tell her John what special Friday this is."

"Tonight is Good Friday," John answered from the back seat.

"See?" Luke smiled as he watched Jenny in his rearview mirror. "You learned something tonight. Now, I'm going to give you a test - a very important test. If you pass, maybe we'll let you go. Tell me why all good Christians celebrate Good Friday?"

"It has something to do with Easter," Jenny said nervously, not really sure what Good Friday was or why these boys were tormenting her. At least, no one had hurt her - not yet.

"You're not sure, are you?" Luke taunted her.

"Not exactly," Jenny admitted. She was trying to figure out where the boys were taking her. They seemed to be driving around aimlessly in Highland Park.

"Matt, tell our little Jewish friend what Good Friday commemorates," Luke ordered.

"It's the day that Jesus Christ was crucified."

"Right on Matt." Luke continued his interrogation. "What's your name little girl?"

"Jenny." She noticed her voice was trembling. Her whole body was shivering. "Please let me go." Tears were streaming down her cheeks.

"Take her home, Luke. We scared her enough," Pete said.

"Look chicken Pete. Just shut up. You lost the bet, so this is my show," Luke said angrily. He looked at the girl. "Now Jenny, you didn't pass the first test, but to show you what a good sport I am, I'm going to give you another test - another chance. Tell us who killed Christ?" Luke watched in the mirror as Jenny dried her eyes.

"The Romans, I think," Jenny said between sobs.

"Well, you're almost right," Luke conceded. "The Romans did it, but do you know why?"

Jenny was silent.

"I'll tell you why little Jew girl. The Jews told them to kill Jesus. The Jews screamed for His blood. It's all in the Bible, the whole story. That's why everyone hates the Jews. Didn't you know that? How stupid can you be not to know the Jews killed Christ?" Luke grabbed the can of beer that Pete was holding and took a big swallow.

Jenny noticed they were driving north on Green Bay Road, past the turnoff to the hospital. Soon they would be in Highwood, the Little Italy of the North Shore with its dozens of quaint restaurants and bars.

"Do you know what it feels like to be on the cross?" Luke's tone was not teasing anymore. It was ugly. He was mad. Mad at the Jews for killing his Lord. Mad at all the Jews. And he had one young Jewish girl in the back seat of his car, helpless and in his power.

The red Toyota glided to a stop in front of St. Christopher's Catholic Church of Highwood, Illinois. The church was dark. Services were over. In the courtyard, set far back from the street behind a wrought iron fence was a lovely garden. In the center of the garden, on a marble pedestal, was a life-size sculpture of Jesus on the cross.

Luke turned around and faced Jenny. "We're taking you out of the car now little Jew girl. There is no one around, but if you open your mouth to scream, I'll smash your face in. All those pretty white teeth will go right down your throat. You understand?"

"Please don't hurt me," Jenny begged. Her whole body was trembling as the boys pulled her out of the car and marched her into the courtyard. They pushed her up against Jesus on the cross. Luke took out the clothesline from the brown paper bag that Pete had bought at White Hen. Matt and John lifted Jenny up while Luke tied her arms to the cold stone cross. Luke cut the rope with his pocket knife and then tied Jenny's feet to the bottom of the cross. The boys let go and Jenny sagged on the cross, her weight straining against the ropes around her arms.

"Please get me down! My arms are killing me," Jenny cried out in pain.

"Now you know how Jesus felt," Luke taunted her.

"But I didn't kill Him! Why are you torturing me? I never hurt anyone in my whole life."

"You're a Jew. That's why," Luke replied as if the answer were self-evident.

"Okay Luke, you had your fun. Now let's get her down and get out of here," Pete demanded.

"It doesn't look right," Luke said ignoring his friend. The boys stepped back and looked at twelve year-old

Jenny Sanders crying hysterically as she hung from the cross in the courtyard of St. Christopher's.

"Oh God please help me," Jenny sobbed.

"That's the problem little Jew girl. You got the wrong God. No one can help you now," Luke laughed as he watched Jenny struggle helplessly against the ropes tying her to the cross.

"I know what's wrong," Luke said triumphantly. "Jesus was stripped before they nailed Him to the cross."

"Oh for Christ's sake Luke, that's enough already," Pete protested.

"Go bring us some beer Pete and stop being such a Jew-lover."

Luke climbed the steps to the cross. Jenny looked up at the tall muscular young man.

"Please get me down. My arms are breaking. I promise I won't tell. Please let me go. Please!" Jenny cried.

Luke unzipped Jenny's jacket and pulled it open. He watched her small breasts heave up and down against the thin cotton fabric of her blouse. Luke placed his hands on Jenny's breasts and then he tore open her lavender blouse and ripped off her bra. In one fast motion he undid her jeans and pulled them down with her panties to the ropes around her ankles. The boys stared at her naked slim body. Her white skin glistened with sweat.

"Oh God, please help me. Help me somebody," Jenny whimpered in fright and shame.

Luke got the new six-pack of Coors from Pete and carried it up to the cross.

"You guys want to help cleanse a Jew?" Luke laughed. His friends just watched as Luke opened the cans of beer and poured them over Jenny's head and body. He massaged her breasts and moved his big hands lustfully up and down her thighs.

"I bet you're still a virgin aren't you Jenny?" Luke said as he squeezed her nipples until she screamed in pain. Luke quickly clapped his hand over her mouth. "Remember what I told you Jew girl. No noise or you'll lose all your teeth," Luke snarled at her. "Bet you guys never saw a virgin screwed on a cross before."

"Holy Jesus, that's enough Luke." Pete ran up the steps and pulled Luke away from Jenny. Luke shoved him down the steps.

"She's mine and I'll do anything I want with her," Luke yelled at his friends, obviously very drunk.

"No you won't, you big ape!"

The boys whirled around and saw a priest dash up the steps and stand in front of Jenny. Father Dominick Salvatore, a seventy-year-old Jesuit priest was not going to let those hoodlums hurt the young girl crying on the cross.

"Aw come on Father, you gotta be kidding," Luke said as the boys encircled the old priest who was only a few inches taller than Jenny. "I could crush you with one hand tied behind my back," Luke boasted.

"Then you'll have to do it," Father Dominick said. "And if you touch me or that girl, you'll burn in Hell forever."

"Father, she's just a Jew girl, a Christ killer," Luke protested.

"And you are a stupid ass. Who do you think Jesus' mother was?"

"The Virgin Mary," Luke mumbled.

"And don't you know that Mary was a Jewess and Jesus was a Jew?

"Jesus was a Jew," Luke repeated dumbly.

"You boys get out of here and take your drunken friend with you. And leave me the knife," the priest ordered.

Luke dropped his knife and ran back to the car with his friends. The red Toyota sped away.

Father Dominick cut the ropes binding Jenny to the cross. She collapsed in his arms. The old priest pulled up her jeans, zipped her jacket and helped her into the rectory.

"What's all the commotion about?" Mrs. Bellino appeared at the door in her bathrobe. She had been housekeeper for Father Dominick for twenty years.

"Oh my God," she said as she rushed to help Jenny.

"She smells like you pulled her out of a keg of beer."

"Give her a warm shower and put her to bed. We'll talk to her later when she calms down a little." Father Dominick kissed Jenny on the forehead. "You'll be fine, my child. You're in safe hands now and you'll be home very soon."

Father Dominick hurried to his office to call the police.

Chapter

Two

Professor Benjamin Sanders and his wife Michelle were celebrating. Tonight was special. Across the table, the candlelight cast a soft glow on Michelle - still lovely to look at and bright to be with. Tonight marked six months that Ben's fourth novel, *Naked Truth*, was on the *New York Times* Best Seller List. Herb and Betty Wolf were supposed to join them tonight, but Betty got sick. Ben was happy to be alone with Michelle. Life was sweet for the Sanders family.

It wasn't always that way. They had married right after they both graduated from the University of Chicago. Ben received a fellowship to work on his Ph.D. in History and Michelle took a job as a sales broker for Glencoe Realty. After two years as a childless couple, they decided to start a family.

That's when the trouble started. Michelle couldn't get pregnant or stay pregnant for more than a few weeks. For six years the specter of being childless hung over them like a dark angry cloud. Tears soaked their pillows many nights when they talked of the child they so desperately wanted, but could not have. Costly injections of Pergonal and Clomid pills, three in vitros did not work. Even Ben's appointment as Assistant Professor of History at Lake Forest College did little to cheer them.

Then came the miracle. Dr. Alan Burns of Chicago Medical School discovered a new technique to help infertile couples. He found that Ben and Michelle had a blood incompatibility.

Ben enjoyed teaching. Helping students discover the past as a guide to the future. But he wanted more. His vivid imagination was restless in the confines of facts and antiquity. Ben started writing mystery novels for fun and money. "To *Naked Truth*," Ben raised his wine glass and gently clinked Michelle's glass.

"To *Naked Truth* and my favorite husband," Michelle responded.

"I wonder how Jenny's doing at Gloria's?"

"Ben, you worry all the time. You have to learn to let go. Jenny is a big girl now."

Ben sipped his wine and continued on his favorite subject, their daughter. "No more running down the hall half-naked or crawling into bed with us at night to watch TV."

"Face it dear. Jenny can't be Daddy's little girl forever."

"I know, but I do miss all those hugs and kisses."

"Don't worry. Jenny's Mom will still take good care of you."

"Is that a promise?"

"Cross my heart," Michelle smiled.

"I have a sudden urge to go home to our nice empty house," Ben said eagerly.

"No dessert?'

"Let's have dessert at home, in bed", Ben smiled.

"Ben, you've been reading too many of your books with those fantasy sex scenes you dream up."

"You're my inspiration darling."

The Sanders drove from the Wildfire Restaurant to their white colonial home on Linden Lane in Highland Park. They were quiet in the car surrounded by the exciting melodies of Rachmaninoff's *Second Piano Concerto* from their CD deck. The house was dark except for the single hall light they had left on. As they climbed the stairs to their bedroom, they could hear the beep from the answering machine.

"Let's ignore it," Ben teased.

"I can't Ben. It could be the Millers finally ready to make an offer on the house I showed them six times."

"You promised me dessert remember." Ben put his arms around Michelle's still slim waist.

She slipped away. "I'll just be a minute. Keep those hormones flowing."

Michelle smiled at the fun she and Ben still had after eighteen years of marriage.

Michelle pushed the message button.

"My name is Father Dominick from St. Christopher's Catholic Church in Highwood."

The voice was calm and controlled.

"Didn't we give them some clothes for their auction last year?" Ben called out as he started to undress.

"Shh! Let me hear."

"Don't be alarmed. Jenny is not hurt. She is resting in our rectory. She's waiting for you. There was an incident outside of the church this evening."

Michelle and Ben rushed to their car and sped to Highwood.

Father Dominick answered the bell immediately. He quickly led Jenny's parents to a small bedroom on the first floor. Jenny was in bed, curled into a little ball. A bright floral quilt covered her.

Mrs. Bellino was holding her hand and gently stroking her long black hair. Michelle rushed to her daughter, took her into her arms and cradled her like a baby. Jenny clung to her mother and started sobbing uncontrollably. The priest led Ben outside the room and explained what had happened.

"How could they do such a thing Father? What kind of animals were those boys?"

"Drunk animals Mr. Sanders. Drunk with beer and lust. I gave the police all the information including a description of the car. They'll catch them."

"They better be caught. They'll be safer in jail than they will be on the street if I ever get my hands on them." Ben was surprised at his words. He had never threatened anyone in his life. Now he was ready to kill.

Chapter

Three

It is true. Time heals. For weeks after the attack, Jenny would not go out alone. Michelle would drive her to school and pick her up. At night she crawled into bed with her parents to feel safe.

Sexual abuse had been in the headlines for weeks, but Ben and Michelle never thought it would happen to their daughter. They encouraged Jenny to confide her feelings and fears so they could comfort her and surround her with their love.

Ben wanted to strangle those boys for what they did to his daughter. Sure the judge would give them a sentence, a slap on the wrist. But Ben wanted them to suffer, to feel the pain they had inflicted on Jenny and on her parents. How could he do that? Who could he hire to beat up those boys? Now he understood Chicago's gang warfare. The gangs did not wait for justice from the courts. They dealt out their own justice: murder for murder.

Having those boys beaten bloody by some hired thugs would satisfy Ben's rage, but what good would it do? The source of their hate would remain untouched. Ben decided to let the courts do their job. He would find the source for their hate and expose it to the world.

One night at the dinner table Jenny asked her father: "Why did those boys hate Jews so much that they did those awful things to me?"

"Jenny, babies don't hate anyone. Children have to be taught to hate. Unfortunately, the Christian Bible says many hateful, untrue things about the Jews. The strange thing is that the center of Christianity is a Jew, Jesus Christ, who is said to be the son of God and preached that we should all love one another. Sadly, those boys learned from comments by their parents and their minister that the Jews were an evil people. When the Gospel of John was read in church, they were told by the Holy Bible that Jews were children of the Devil. If the Jews were children of the Devil any punishment was acceptable.

"But what did the Jews do to make them believe that?" Jenny asked.

"The New Testament claims that the Jews killed Jesus Christ, their God."

"Did they?"

"No Jenny. The Jews didn't kill Jesus, the Romans did that, but some Jews did want the Romans to do it. However, the New Testament blames all the Jews for all time to be guilty of killing Jesus."

"But that's not fair," Jenny protested.

"Of course, it is not fair. And millions of Jews died because of that lie."

"And that's why those boys attacked me? For something that happened thousands of years ago? That is just so stupid!"

"You are so right Jenny. Hatred of the Jews is stupid and has been going on for centuries. Anti-Semitism is a creation of Christianity."

"Well you better set them straight with your book."

"I will certainly try. Now, let's help Mom with the dishes and get you ready for school tomorrow."

Jenny started to leave the table to help her Mom in the kitchen and then sat back down.

"One more question?" Jenny asked.

"Okay," Ben replied. Jenny was great at asking questions usually to delay her bedtime.

"Why didn't God help me when I was crying for His help?"

"That's a tough one Jenny. Many believe that God does not intervene in the affairs of mankind. That God gave man free will to make his own decisions. Others might say that God enabled Father Dominick to hear your screams so he could come and rescue you. That is a question that has disturbed many people for ages, especially about the Holocaust. I'm afraid that is a question you will have to work out for yourself, but not tonight. Let's go help Mom."

Slowly confidence returned. Jenny began to play with her friends, gossip on the phone, prepare for her Bat Mitzvah.

The boys were caught the day after the attack on Jenny. In a plea bargain, John, Matt and Pete were given one year probation and one hundred hours of community service. Luke was sentenced to two years in jail. With good behavior, he would be out in six months.

For Ben, the attack on Jenny was a continuing nightmare. How could such a horror happen to his precious daughter? Could it happen again? Why did those boys hate Jews so much that they would terrorize Jenny? Where did all that hate come from? Not from Jesus, the Prince of Peace. Not from Father Dominick who saved Jenny from those hoodlums. Every night Ben worked on his new book.

There had to be an answer and Ben would find it. When he did, he sent his manuscript to his agent, Michael Morris. Several days later, Ben had an appointment to discuss his latest project with his agent.

"The New Testament is a lie! Are you crazy? How do you expect me to sell that?" Michael Morris shoved the manuscript across his desk to Ben. Michael puffed on his long Garcia & Vega cigar and watched with amusement as his client waved the smoke away.

"I write them and you sell them. That's our deal."

"Sure that's our deal Ben, but I need the right merchandise. Your last book, *Naked Truth,* now that was merchandise I could sell. Sex, murder, bondage – it had everything the public wants. That was a pushover. You've got a name now Ben. Don't screw it up with this serious religious stuff. There's no market for it. No money. Forget it. Go home and dream up a nice, weird murder mystery.

Have a daughter go bananas and rape her little brother or have some sweet old librarian become a mass murderer. That I can sell."

"Michael, I'm tired of writing all that junk. I want to do something important. Something I can really be proud of."

"You can be proud of *Naked Truth*. Six months on the *New York Times* Best Seller List. That's money in the bank, wonderful family, nice home, what more do you want?"

"I want to change the world, Michael. I want to scream about all the hate and violence. I want people to listen to the truth."

"Ben, you want a soapbox. I'll give you a soapbox. Go downstairs to Grant Park and scream all the truth you want. I'm a salesman. I sell books to publishers. I'm damn good. I know my business. This won't sell. Forget it. Go home. Count your money and come back with *Naked Truth Two*. That I can sell."

"Michael, do me a favor. Find me a publisher, a little boutique shop. This book is important to me. Forget the money. We both made enough on *Naked Truth*."

Ben pushed the manuscript back across the desk. "Anyone can sell what the public wants. A real salesman can sell what the public needs."

"What the public needs is some fun, some laughs. Not many laughs in the Bible. I'll check around Ben, but don't hold your breath."

Ben stood up, shook hands with his agent and quickly left the world of commerce for the more serene world of academia. Of course he wanted a soapbox, but a mass media soapbox that would electrify the world.

Michael Morris swiveled his chair around to the window. The Chicago skyline curved along the restless lake. A beautiful view. A bustling city. A vibrant city. Everyone out hustling for a buck. The whites, the blacks, the Poles, the Jews, the Mexicans, the Italians, the Koreans, the Indians, the Chinese. Chicago had them all. Everyone working, sweating, dreaming. Some fighting, stealing, raping. The very rich and the very poor. Only blocks apart and worlds apart.

Michael was on top. A highly respected literary agent in the Midwest. The big fish in a little pond. Chicago wasn't New York or Los Angeles, but there was plenty of talent here. Michael could recognize talent and he could sell it.

Benjamin Sanders was his prize find. A history professor at Lake Forest College with an itch to write murder mysteries. Five years ago, Ben brought him a psychological thriller about a student's almost perfect crime. Michael sold it to Bantam Books and Ben had a new career.

Ben's fourth novel, *Naked Truth* was a blockbuster. The public was clamoring for more. What does Ben do with his precious time? He wastes it on this Bible stuff. Now who in hell wants to read about *The Trial of St. John?*

Michael relit his cigar. Muriel did not like him to smoke. Bad for his health. Bad for her health.

It didn't hurt Muriel. A drunk driver killed her. Swerved across the center lane on Lake Shore Drive and hit her head on. She never had a chance. That was three years ago. Michael was alone. Their two sons married and moved away. Michael sold his big house in Glencoe and moved into the Trump Tower, fiftieth floor, fabulous view overlooking the Chicago River and Lake Michigan.

So here he was, fifty-five years old, successful and alone. His newest project: sell a Bible story to a public ready to feast on a steady diet of sex and murder. Well, it was a challenge and certainly an interesting book. He owed Ben a try after all the juicy commissions from *Naked Truth*.

Michael flipped through his smart phone and punched a number.

"Sandra, this is Michael Morris. How's my favorite publisher today?"

"Michael Morris! Business must be terrible if you're calling me. You know I don't do sex, at least not for my books."

"That's a great opening Sandra. Perhaps we should explore it someday."

"Anytime, Michael. You know I fantasize about you every day just about this time."

"Seriously Sandra, I have a special book that is perfect for you."

"Since when have you given up ax-murders and sex orgies? Have you made so much on *Naked Truth* that you can afford to get involved in literature?"

"Now Sandra, don't knock my bread and butter. But *Naked Truth* is what I want to talk to you about.

The author, you know Benjamin Sanders, just gave me a serious book that needs your special touch."

"No sex. No murders?" Sandra asked suspiciously.

"Only one murder, but a very important one."

"How important?"

"The most famous, most tragic murder in the history of the world."

"Jesus!" Sandra exclaimed.

"You guessed it, Jesus. Why don't we talk over dinner tonight?"

"For you Michael, I'll cancel my date with the handsome Prince of Morocco."

"He's dead."

"So is my love life."

"I'll pick you up at seven."

"Can't wait."

Michael smiled, hung up the phone and picked up the manuscript on his desk. Who knows? Maybe he could do it. Maybe he could sell this Jesus story. Of course, it could be dangerous if he did. Salman Rushdie was still in hiding from the Muslim fanatics for *Satanic Verses*. There were Christian fanatics out there who would crucify anyone tampering with the New Testament. Well, Ben must know he's playing with fire. If that's what he wants, why not try?

Michael Morris smiled across the table. His temples were streaked with grey, accenting his wavy black hair. His custom-made navy silk suit draped perfectly over his stocky frame.

"L'Chaim," he said, clinking glasses with Sandra at a window table in the Camellia Room at the Drake Hotel.

"L'Chaim," she smiled back. Sandra Price was an outrageous flirt and the sole owner of Harborside Press since her husband died twelve years ago. She published poetry, non-fiction and a few serious novels. Nothing flashy. Good solid titles for a limited market that wanted to read what she liked.

Sandra was petite, pretty and still had a nice figure. She was seventy-two and as mentally alert as when she seduced her students at South Shore High to fall in love with Shakespeare, Browning and Alexander Pope.

"Michael, this must be a hard sell. The Camella Room and champagne. I feel like it's Prom Night."

"Tell me about Prom Night."

"Ancient history, Michael. Back then, in the Dark Ages, most girls were virgins when they got married, divorce was a scandal and drugs were medicines you took if you got sick. The most violence we ever had at school was a fist fight over a girl or a football score. Nowadays, children have babies, fathers vanish, drugs turn kids into zombies and you can get shot anywhere, anytime just minding your own business. It's a scary world, Michael."

"It certainly is. And Sandra, you have a chance to change it."

"By publishing Ben's book? I'm going to stop the killing and the hate?"

"It might help. Why are you still in this business Sandra?"

"I like it. It's fun. I want to give people good books to read."

"Why? Why bother? I'll tell you why. Because books make a difference. It's a one-on-one relationship. Author to reader. Just the two of them, alone in the world the author created. And sometimes, the author touches someone's soul and makes a difference in their life."

The waiter appeared discretely at their table. Sandra looked and smiled at the young man. "You're just in time. I'm famished."

"How do you to it, Sandra?"

"Do what?"

"Stay so slim. You eat like a Bears fullback.'

"Exercise."

"What kind of exercise?"

"Lovemaking. I give a course to all my young authors, male and female."

"Sandra, you are shameless," Michael laughed.

"I know. But talk is cheap. And no one ever got HIV from conversation."

Michael gave Sandra a quick summary of Ben's book while they enjoyed their dinner. "So what do you think about Ben's idea? Will the public buy it?"

"Maybe. I'll read the manuscript you sent over and call you in a few days. If it is as good as you say, it could sell, but it might be too hot to handle. His book could offend a lot of people, very powerful people."

"Does that bother you, Sandra? Controversy is what ignites a best seller. You're too tough to be scared. What's really going on?"

"This is strictly confidential, Michael. I've had an offer, a really good offer to sell Harborside Press. I don't want to screw it up by taking on some very controversial book."

"Who's the offer from? My lips are sealed, promise."

"From Gerald Crane."

"Gerald Crane. He's come a long way. I knew him when he was Jerry Cohen. Name was too Jewish for him. He wanted to blend in."

"Oh, he's blended in all right," Sandra replied. "His Chicago Media Group owns twelve neighborhood newspapers and three FM stations."

"Tell you what Sandra. If you like Ben's book, you have permission to show it to dear old Gerald. I can give you a week to decide before I show this next best seller to someone else."

"Michael, your favors are endless."

"Only for you love."

"Take me home Michael before I turn into a pumpkin. This has been such fun."

Michael parked in the driveway of the Astor street condo building and walked Sandra to the door. She looked at him wistfully and kissed him on the cheek.

"Thank you Michael. It was a lovely evening. I'd ask you up, but frankly, you're too old for me."

"You don't know what you're missing," Michael smiled back.

"That's the problem Michael. I do. Goodnight."

Sandra Price disappeared into the ornate lobby.

Chapter

Four

MICHELLE WAS NERVOUS. SHE sensed trouble. Life was too sweet. It was like basking in the sunshine knowing a thunderstorm was lurking just beyond the horizon. How could life be better? She loved her husband and he loved her, passionately, thank heavens. And Jenny was the answer to all their prayers. Now that Ben was a successful author, money was no longer a problem. If only their life could stay this way, but Michelle was worried about the new book.

Ben seemed obsessed with it. If only he would stick to his clever murder mysteries and erotic sex scenes. But no, her dear, darling professor had to dig and probe and search and study everything known to man about the murder of Jesus two thousand years ago. For what? To prove the New Testament was wrong? That the Jews were falsely accused of killing Jesus? What does it matter? The Holocaust is over. The gas chambers are museum pieces.

We can't bring back the dead. Michelle feared *The Trial of St. John* might turn into a nightmare.

The Sanders family settled in the book-lined den. Michelle snuggled up to her husband on the couch. Jenny and Dutchess played tug-of-war with an old sock. From the picture window overlooking their spacious yard, the first buds of spring had come to life on the old maple tree. Springtime, the resurrection of life from the death of winter. The time for Passover and Easter. A year since the attack on Jenny.

"So professor, how did dear old Michael like your manuscript?"

Michelle had waited until they were comfortably settled in the den to get the news.

Either way, she would lose. If the book was published, she would worry about possible violent repercussions. If it wasn't published, all of Ben's hard work and research would have been in vain. A year spent in the 1st Century with no audience to share his discoveries. This was an important book, a vaccine against hate. She would rather suffer the consequences than see Ben's hopes and dreams shattered. It was his defense of Jenny, his earnest effort to protect her future. "Michael didn't think he could sell it. He'd rather I do *Naked Truth Two* or something like it. But he has contacts. He said he would try."

"I know how hard you worked on the book Ben, but I'm scared."

"I know. I am too." Ben put his arm around Michelle and pulled her onto his lap. He kissed her gently on the lips. He longed to feel more of her, but Jenny was there. Jenny squeezed between her parents and kissed them both.

"OK you two lovebirds. Are you going to feed your starving daughter or do I sue for child abuse?"

"Oh you poor dear." Michelle gave her a love pat on her bottom and disappeared into the kitchen.

"Now I got you all to myself," Jenny laughed and gave her father a big hug.

"You are a little troublemaker Jenny"

"I know. But you love it don't you?"

"Of course, I do."

"Daddy, guess what?"

"What?"

"I got the part."

"What part?"

"Cinderella. Don't you remember? Auditions were today."

"Of course you got the part. You're the prettiest girl in the whole school."

"Maybe you're a little biased," Jenny laughed.

"OK. Now tell me Cinderella, how did you get the part?"

"Well, our auditions were in front of our drama teacher and the whole class. Mrs. Thomas picked me and two other girls to play a scene with the Prince. And guess what?"

"What?"

"Guess who the Prince was?"

"George Clooney?"

"Silly. He's too old. The Prince was Bobby Stein. He's gorgeous and I'm in love."

"So soon?"

"OK. I'm really not in love yet, but I could be. He's really a sweet boy."

"I thought you didn't like boys."

"A woman can change her mind can't she?"

"So what scene did you do?"

"The mushy one at the ball. Where Cinderella kisses the Prince and runs away and loses her shoe."

"So what happened?"

"I wanted to be last so I told Mrs. Thomas I had to go to the bathroom, but I really didn't. I went out of the auditorium and then peeked through the door to see how the other girls did. Sally MacKenzie kissed the Prince on the cheek, giggled and ran away. Karen Greenberg didn't giggle, but she's much taller than Bobby and had to bend over to kiss him. It looked funny."

"So what did you do?"

"I ran back to the stage, read the part and gave Bobby a big kiss on his lips. The kids all loved it and clapped. Poor Bobby, he just blushed like crazy."

"You little vixen. That poor boy doesn't have a chance."

"I know. Come on, let's eat. Mom's calling us." Jenny pulled on her Dad's arm to help him off the couch.

"Nice of you to help your old father now that there's a new man in your life."

"Oh Daddy. It's just a play."

"And how many other boys have you kissed young lady?" Michelle asked with mock seriousness.

"You were eavesdropping Mom."

"Of course I was. That's what mothers do. It's in our contract."

"Bobby's the first boy I ever kissed. I liked it."

As the family sat around the dining room table, Ben thought: "How exciting to watch his little girl grow up. How dangerous to have a beautiful, young daughter in a world full of maniacs."

"Hey Pop. Your soup's getting cold. What are you daydreaming about?"

"Your wedding Cinderella. Now that you found your Prince, we better make out the wedding list."

"Oh Daddy! It was just one kiss."

Chapter

Five

SANDRA PRICE CALLED HER office precisely at 9 a.m. She knew Elizabeth would be there. For twenty-two years Elizabeth was always there, on time, cheerful. Sandra couldn't run Harborside Press without her.

"Good morning. Harborside Press."

"Good morning, Elizabeth"

"Good morning, Mrs. Price."

"Elizabeth, I have a new manuscript to read. I'll be home today. Just hold my calls."

"Of course, Mrs. Price. I hope you found a winner for us."

"Might be. I'll let you know."

Sandra disconnected her phone. She liked to read without interruptions. To concentrate totally on what the author was trying to say. She went to her old oak desk in the sitting room. The morning sun over Lake Michigan sent golden shafts of warmth through her windows. She pulled the manuscript out of the envelope Michael Morris had given her. The title page read:

THE TRIAL OF ST. JOHN

By Benjamin J. Sanders

Sandra felt the warmth of the sun on her neck and the excitement of a new manuscript in her hands. Sandra knew she held the hopes and dreams of an author. Now it was just a pile of papers. If Sandra Price said yes, it could become a book. Perhaps is would become a book to be found in libraries around the world, to be studied at universities, to be treasured in thousands of private homes.

Of the hundreds of manuscripts submitted to Harborside Press, only a few were chosen to be read personally by Sandra Price. As a favor to Michael Morris, Sandra would read *The Trial of St. John* herself instead of giving it to one of her editors. She turned the page to CHAPTER ONE.

The Trial of St. John

CHAPTER ONE

THE COURTROOM WAS FILLED. The large crowd was silent. The Prosecutor was terribly thin with dark sunken eyes. He wore the striped prison uniform of Auschwitz. He had torn sandals on his feet and no socks. His bony ankles and bare toes were clearly visible. His voice was soft almost a whisper.

He looked at the proud figure in the witness box. A tall man, clean-shaven and handsomely garbed in a white Roman toga.

"Are you John the Gospel writer?" the Prosecutor asked.

"I am."

"John, you write of the crucifixion as if you were an eyewitness. Were you actually there?"

"Of course not. I was born seventy years after our Lord Jesus was crucified."

"Then how do you know that your account is accurate?"

"I learned about Jesus Christ from the writings of Paul, Mark, Matthew, Luke and others."

"What others?" the Prosecutor demanded.

"There were many accounts of Jesus. He was such an incredible personality that those who knew Him and His miracles spoke of Him years after His crucifixion. Some of their stories were written down. Unfortunately, most have been lost with the passage of time."

"Could you explain why your story of Jesus is so different from the Gospels of Mark, Matthew and Luke?"

They were not eyewitnesses either. We each had our sources. Naturally, over time as stories are passed from generation to generation they may vary. I selected the stories I thought most credible."

"Did you ever doubt the accuracy of your sources?"

"Of course I did. But the purpose of my Gospel was not to give a precise history, but to instill faith. To bring the message of Jesus Christ to the Roman world."

"Would you alter the story of Jesus a bit if you thought it would further your cause?" the Prosecutor asked as he approached John in the witness chair.

"The story had to be told in a way acceptable to the Roman authorities."

The Prosecutor paced slowly in front of the judge and the witness. The Judge was dressed in the purple robe of a Roman jurist. His face was leathery from years as an

Army commander. His features were sharp, eyes alert, his curly hair was pure white.

"Let me rephrase the question," the Prosecutor said as he walked back to the witness box.

"Would you invent part of your Gospel if it would help your cause?"

"Of course I would."

There was a murmur throughout the crowd. The Judge banged his gavel.

"There must be quiet in the courtroom," the judge ordered in a deep, resonant voice.

The Prosecutor moved closer to the witness box.

"In other words John, part of your Gospel, part of the New Testament may not actually be true. Events may not have happened exactly as you described, is that correct?"

"You don't understand. The times were terrible."

John turned to the Judge. "Your honor, may I read from my notes? It will help explain the plight of the early Christians."

"You may do so John. Mr. Prosecutor, why don't you sit down while John presents his part of the story."

The Prosecutor walked slowly back to his chair and slid silently into it like a shadow dissolving in the light.

John described the torment of the early Christians. By refusing to accept the gods of Rome, thousands died to affirm their faith in Jesus Christ. Christians were forced to face lions and tigers in the Coliseum in Rome. The Romans cheered as the followers of Jesus were torn limb from limb by the wild beasts.

When John finished, the Prosecutor rose from his chair and approached the witness stand. There were tears in his eyes.

"Brutality is sinful in all ages. The Christians were martyrs. They died for their beliefs."

John nodded his head. "They surely did," he said chocking back his tears.

The Prosecutor paced slowly in front of the witness box.

"John, you and the other Gospel authors portray Pontius Pilate as a kind, compassionate Governor. He really wanted to free Jesus. It was those terrible Jews that demanded that Jesus be crucified. That portrayal does not fit the historical record we have of Pontius Pilate from Josephus and other eyewitnesses. According to them, Pilate was a cruel Governor who squeezed the Jews mercilessly for taxes, crucified hundreds before and after Jesus and finally was recalled to Rome because of reports of his excessive brutality."

John shifted in his chair. He replied forcefully to the Prosecutor.

"And what do you think would have happened to our Christian movement if we wrote about a Roman Governor the way you suggest?" His voice was firm and righteous.

John continued: "You don't understand how it was in our time. Rome was master of the world, our world. Roman legions enforced Roman law from England to North Africa. France, Spain, Egypt, Greece, Syria, Judea,

Turkey were all part of the huge Roman Empire. The Mediterranean was a Roman Sea.

"Of all the conquered peoples, the Jews were the most rebellious. They kept praying for a Messiah to lead them in battle against the Romans."

John continued his testimony. "There were constant Jewish uprisings that the Romans crushed. Some suggested that Jesus was a rebel leader who came to Jerusalem to lead a revolt against the Romans. Pontius Pilate may have had that in mind when he put the sign on the Cross: 'King of the Jews.' That would show the Jews what happened to enemies of Rome."

The Prosecutor sighed, "I do understand. I know what brutes men can be."

"May I continue?" John asked, peeved at the interruption.

John looked at his notes. "In 66 AD the Jews attacked and captured a Roman fort in the Galilee. The Romans sent in huge reinforcements to put down the revolt. For five years the war raged across Judea. After a long siege and fierce battles, the Romans conquered Jerusalem in 70 AD. Josephus estimates a million Jews died in the battle for Jerusalem, most from starvation and disease.

"The Romans completely destroyed the magnificent Temple that had been lavishly rebuilt by King Herod. The Jews were totally crushed. Thousands were taken to Rome in chains and marched before cheering crowds before they were executed or thrown to the lions in the Coliseum.

"The Jewish people and their precious Torah had been battered into oblivion by the awesome might of the Roman Empire. That is the world we lived in when the Gospels were written. Of course we portrayed the Romans in a kinder light than they deserved. What else could we do if we wanted to survive? What harm would it do the Jews if we blamed them? They were crushed already. We expected the Jews to vanish into history."

The Prosecutor jumped to his feet. "What harm did it do?" he shouted. "We didn't disappear. We survived despite you." The Prosecutor was trembling with rage. "Look at me," he demanded. "You did this to me. You killed millions of us through the centuries. The Crusades, the Inquisition, the pogroms, the Holocaust. Rivers of Jewish blood. Why? Because the Jews killed Jesus. The Christ killers deserved to die. It was a lie and you knew it!

"Jesus was a Jewish rabbi. All his disciples were Jewish. All his followers were Jewish. Most of His wonderful teachings came from Isiah and Ezekiel, from Moses and Hillel. Jesus preached in synagogues. He loved the Jewish people and died a Jewish hero. But you changed the story. You made the Roman tyrant a kindly gentleman who washed his hands of the whole ugly affair. You made the Jews guilty of killing Jesus. For God's sake, why couldn't you have told the truth?

"The Jews killed Jesus? What Jews? Who were they? You didn't write that the Jewish High Priest was paid by Rome and could be fired by Rome. That the Jewish priestly establishment were collaborators with Rome to keep peace in Judea and keep their positions of power.

"When Jesus entered Jerusalem he was heralded by huge crowds. Many thought he was the Messiah they had been praying for to lead them against the Roman tyrants. These Jews did not want Jesus killed. The crowds that greeted Jesus were not the Jews in the courtyard of Pontius Pilate. Jesus was a popular leader, a faith healer. Jesus was arrested in the middle of the night while his followers were asleep. The High Priest and the Romans feared the public would rebel if they seized Jesus during daylight.

"The Jews in Pilate's courtyard shouting "crucify Him" were the priests, the collaborators, the paid friends of Rome. Pontius Pilate murdered Jesus to get rid of another Jewish troublemaker. The priests wanted Jesus killed because he had defied the authority of the Temple hierarchy.

"But you sir," the Prosecutor pointed his bony finger at John, "you made all the Jews for all time the killers of Jesus Christ, the killers of your God.

"God only knows how much blood has been spilled because you damned us forever as Christ killers. How could you do it? How could you?"

The Prosecutor returned to his chair. He put his head down on the table and wept. His muffled cries echoed in the courtroom.

The judge banged his gavel. "We will adjourn until tomorrow at 10 AM." The first day of the trial was over.

Sandra Price put the manuscript down. The sun had left the sitting room. She felt chilled and sad and excited. How could you criticize the Bible? The Holy Book. God's Word. Over the centuries, thousands of men and women had died for their faith in Jesus.

Who would buy such a book? If she published it, what would it mean for Harborside Press? Would there be boycotts, pickets, threats? America, thank heavens is a free country, but it is overwhelmingly a Christian country. Should she publish a book that criticizes the Christian Bible in the nation that gave her family refuge from the pogroms in Poland? And what about the crazies out there? Who knows what they might do to her and to Benjamin Sanders for daring to accuse St. John of betraying the spirit of Jesus Christ?

Chapter

Six

LAIRD HALL WAS ONE of the original buildings on the Lake Forest campus. Leafy green vines in every crevice of the dark red bricks. Preston Laird, a prominent Chicago lawyer, had donated the building to the college in 1899 in memory of his wife. Chiseled over the entrance was the famous quotation from the Gospel of John: "Ye shall know the truth, and the truth shall make you free."

From the open window, Professor Benjamin Sanders could see Lake Michigan hurl itself against the huge boulders of the seawall. Ben often thought of the eternal rhythm of nature. Man was but a puny creature adrift on a twirling ball in the vastness of the universe. The mystery of why and how man was here remained unsolved except for those who believed it was God's will. A more urgent mystery for Ben was why the human passengers on spaceship Earth could not learn to live together in peace and harmony.

Plato, one of Ben's favorite heroes, had a plan for the perfect Republic where men would be ruled by Philosopher-Kings in a realm of Reason. Moses brought the Ten Commandments from God, a guide to live at peace with our neighbors. Jesus taught love for one another and sought to banish hate from the world.

Ben marveled that man had learned to split the atom, walk on the Moon, make millions of calculations per second, unlock the startling mysteries of the genes, make deserts bloom. And yet, Ben knew too well that man, so incredibly intelligent, had still not conquered his passion to destroy his fellow man. Thousands of years after Plato, Moses and Jesus, their messages of reason, faith and love had not changed the conduct of men. Ben thought of this often and pondered what he could do to make the future a little safer, a little saner for Jenny. That's why he wrote *The Trial of St. John* and that's why he was a teacher. Now it was time to stop meditating about the universe and get to the lecture hall.

Ben arranged his notes on the lectern and looked at the students neatly arrayed before him. Unfortunately, there were no assigned seats. He would have put Cindy in the back of the room. Cindy Cunningham always sat in the front row. She was twenty-years-old, bright and vivacious. Her long blonde hair and misty blue eyes reminded him of the early Marilyn Monroe movies. Cindy usually wore a miniskirt to class. She would cross her legs so the soft white flesh of her thighs would shout for Ben's attention. Ben wondered why this should interest him. Michelle was beautiful, his loving wife, and Jenny would hate him if he ever betrayed his family. It must be some primordial male gene that attacks middle-aged men. Ben shifted his thoughts from soft white thighs and young, nubile bodies to the notes on the lectern. His course on Religion in the Western World allowed him to explore his pet theme of the Church versus the Jews.

"Today I'd like to discuss with you the Crusades. From your reading, you know it was not at all like Camelot."

From the darkness of the Crusades, Cindy walked out of class into the bright sunshine of a pleasant, crisp April morning. Cindy and her best friend, Sarah Johnson, sat on a bench watching the waves assault the shoreline.

"Professor Sanders really socked it to the Church this morning," Sarah said.

"He's right. The Church did terrible things. Amazing how religious men, men who believed in Jesus, could be so cruel," Cindy replied.

"Did you see how he looked at you Cindy?"

"I think he has a thing for miniskirts," Cindy laughed.

"That's why I wear them to class. I bet it drives him crazy."

"He is cute isn't he?" Sarah persisted.

"Sure he is. But he's married and as square as they come."

"How do you know that?"

"I took a course in Bible History from him last semester and he never made a pass at me. No invitations to coffee. No private conferences in his office. Nothing."

"Hurts your ego doesn't it," Sarah teased.

"Oh, I could get him in bed if I really tried." Cindy boasted.

"I bet you couldn't," Sarah insisted.

"I could if I wanted to."

"No you couldn't."

"Yes I could."

"How do you know?"

"Because he is a man," Cindy laughed.

"So, you think you could seduce any man?" Sarah asked in amazement.

"I'm sure of it."

"Cindy Cunningham, you must think you're God's gift to mankind."

"Not really. You could have any man you wanted Sarah. You're very pretty and that's all that impresses a guy. They just want a soft body they can get into to prove their manhood."

"What about love?" Sarah asked.

"Love? Love has nothing to do with it. It's strictly biology. Sex is for fun. Love is for life."

"So have you ever done it with a professor?" Sarah persisted.

"No. Have you?"

"Can you keep a secret?"

"Of course, Sarah. What's the secret?"

"I'm still a virgin."

"You're kidding."

"No really. I've never gone to bed with a man. Never met the right guy I guess."

"It's no big deal. Kind of funny really. A lot of pushing and shoving and grunting and groaning."

"Sounds awful."

"It feels good. The guys are grateful. You can have a big football player lick your toes like a pussy cat. Push the right buttons and a man will be like putty in your hands."

Sarah was incensed. "I don't want a man to be like putty. I want a man to be a man. I want to fall in love and have sex only with the man I marry."

"Good luck Sarah. I hope you find him soon. In the meantime, you're missing a lot of fun."

"And I don't have to worry about HIV," Sarah replied.

"I'm very careful. I carry my Trojans with me everywhere. Just in case."

"So, are you going to do it?" Sarah asked.

"Do what?"

"Seduce Professor Sanders."

"Why should I?"

"To prove you could seduce any man you wanted," Sarah teased.

"How much?" Cindy replied, enticed by the challenge.

"What do you mean, how much?" Sarah asked.

"How much would you bet that I could get Professor Sanders in bed with me?"

"You'd do it for money?" Sarah asked in amazement.

"I'd do it for fun. The money would make it like a game."

"OK. Ten bucks."

"Don't be silly. One hundred dollars and I'll do it."

Cindy got off the bench and twirled in front of her friend. Her skirt billowed in the breeze revealing her smooth, long legs. Her golden blonde hair touched her shoulders like a soft caress. Her body tingled with excitement. Of course she could do it. Who could resist such a sweet invitation?

"A hundred dollars is a lot of money," Sarah mused.

"Your Dad's loaded. Tell him you need a new dress. Of course, I could lose and you'd be a hundred dollars richer."

"Think you might lose the bet?"

"It's always possible. Maybe the professor is a saint. Saint Benjamin. But I bet he's just a man. He's got a brain, but he's got a penis too. From what I've seen, what goes on between a man's legs is more important to him that what goes on between his ears."

"Cindy, you're terrible. What an awful thing to say."

"But true."

"How do you know?" Sarah asked, quite amused by her risqué friend.

"I can prove it."

"How?"

"With Professor Sanders. His brain must tell him that sleeping with coeds can only lead to big trouble. But I bet I can raise his penis so high it will lead him straight to my bed."

"Bet you can't."

"Hundred bucks says I can."

"OK. Deal."

The two girls shook hands and giggled.

"How will I know if you do it?" Sarah asked.

"Don't you trust me?"

"Sure I trust you, but for a hundred bucks you should give me proof," Sarah insisted.

"What kind of proof do you want? I can't ask him to pose for pictures."

"How about a hidden recorder or camera?" Sarah suggested.

"I'll think of something."

"Cindy, you're a little devil."

"I know and pretty soon St. Benjamin will know it too."

Chapter
Seven

GERALD CRANE WAS A busy man. His Chicago Media Group of neighborhood newspapers and his FM radio stations had made him a millionaire. It was fun to be rich. To be part of the "in" group of movers and shakers. He could stop working today and have enough money to live handsomely the rest of his life. But what would he do with his time? What could be more exciting, more fun than building an even larger empire?

It wasn't rags to riches, but he could be proud. His father left him the *Hyde Park News* when he died. It was a start, but he had the drive to expand into the suburbs and into radio. He didn't change his name until after his father passed away. Cohen was an honorable name, a privileged name in the Jewish tradition. Crane was neutral. His father would have *plotzed*. He picked the name from his plumbing fixtures. Gerald Crane, named after a toilet. He smiled to himself. Jerry Cohen to Gerald Crane. So simple. Let them guess. With Cohen, they knew for sure. It stuck out like a neon sign: Here is a Jew. Now he blended in. He blended so well he married Nancy Foster of Winnetka. Big church wedding. His two daughters, ages eight and ten, went to the elegant Congregational Church every Sunday with their mother. Gerald didn't go. No big deal. He just didn't go. Maybe there was still some Cohen in him.

Gerald Crane buzzed his secretary, "Dorothy, get me Sandra Price on the phone."

"Right away, Mr. Crane."

In a minute, the line buzzed back. "Hello Sandra. This is Gerald Crane."

"Gerald, how are you?"

"Fine, fine. I'm ready to go with my offer for Harborside Press. Have you talked it over with your lawyer?"

"Lawyers confuse me. They're so picky about everything."

"For your protection, my dear."

"Your offer is fair Gerald. I think I can live with it."

"Good. When can we get together to sign the papers?"

"There is one matter I should tell you about. I'm considering a new manuscript. It is quite controversial."

"I saw your list of coming publications Sandra. They looked fine to me. Just what I need for my Chicago Media Group, a well-known highly respected publishing house."

"This new manuscript wasn't on the list. I just read it yesterday. It may stir up quite a storm."

"What's it about?"

"The crucifixion of Jesus."

"Sounds harmless enough. The libraries are full of Jesus books."

"Not like this one," Sandra replied.

"How so?"

"The author is Benjamin Sanders."

"Terrific. I just finished reading *Naked Truth*. The man is certainly clever. Great plot. Wild sex. So what's the problem?"

"The problem is Ben claims the New Testament is full of lies about the Jews. He claims the Gospels are responsible for anti-Semitism. That the Crusades, the Inquisition, the pogroms, the Holocaust all trace their roots back to the reports in the Bible about the crucifixion of Jesus."

"His book claims the Bible is responsible for all those massacres?" Gerald exclaimed. "I can think of millions of people who would be very angry at anyone criticizing their Bible."

"I know," Sandra replied. "If we publish it, we won't be very popular in the Christian world."

"That is our world Sandra dear. How many books have your Hindu customers bought lately?" Gerald was fuming. "Why don't you just forget it Sandra? Let someone else take the heat."

"I've thought about it."

"So? Just drop it."

"It's really a good book Gerald. I think the public should have a chance to read it."

"Let someone else be the hero Sandra. Don't let this Jesus book screw up our deal."

"I don't think he could find a publisher. Not anyone with real distribution."

"Sandra, this is crazy. You're going to walk away from a ten million dollar deal to publish one '*mashugana*' book?"

"I haven't decided yet."

"Well, when you decide, call me," Gerald said disgusted with this delay in buying Harborside Press.

"Gerald, I want you to read it."

"Why read it? I wouldn't touch it with a ten foot pole. Do you know what a book like that would do to my advertisers? My papers, my radio stations would be crucified if I put my company behind a book that denounces the Holy Bible. For Christ's sake Sandra, use your head. Forget the damn book and take my offer."

"What can it hurt to read it yourself Gerald? I'm going to messenger it over to you today. Just take it home. Turn off your phone and read it. As a favor to an old lady."

"You're no old lady Sandra. You're still a pushy dame. Okay. I'll read the damn book. Send it over."

After dinner, Gerald told his family not to disturb him in the library. He had important work to do. He settled into his favorite leather chair, surveyed his handsome teak paneled hideaway, nodded to the large portrait of his father and took out the manuscript Sandra Price insisted that he read.

The Trial of St. John

CHAPTER TWO

THE PROSECUTOR ARRANGED HIS notes neatly on the table. He walked slowly to the witness box. "Good morning John. This morning I'd like to discuss the Crusades."

"You may discuss all you want Mr. Prosecutor, but I was dead for a thousand years before the Crusades began."

"That is certainly true." A faint smile creased the Prosecutor's thin lips.

"You were indeed dead John, but your Gospel was very much alive. Ever since Emperor Constantine converted to Christianity and sponsored the Council of Nicaea in 325, the Christian religion was changed from a minor persecuted creed to the official state religion of the entire Roman Empire.

"Rome was sacked by the Visigoths in the year 410. Later attacks by Attila the Hun and the Vandals destroyed the rest of the Western Empire. Although the Eastern Empire survived another thousand years, the Roman Empire in Europe collapsed into hundreds of feuding city-states. Only one unifying power was left in all of Europe, the Church. The Pope was the most powerful figure in the Western World, the Emperor of the hereafter.

"Your Gospel was one of the guides for all the Popes. What they did was inspired to a large extent by your words. And your words John condemned the Jews as a sinful people, a people condemned forever because you claimed the Jews killed Jesus Christ.

"In the autumn of 1095, Pope Urban II made a stirring speech before hundreds of nobles and princes assembled at Clermont, France. He called for a Holy Crusade to reclaim Jerusalem from the Muslim Turk infidels. The Turks had been interfering with the profitable trade routes to Asia and had been harassing Christian pilgrims who wanted to visit the Holy places where Jesus was born, preached and died.

"To be sure he could raise a large volunteer army, the Pope promised the serfs freedom from bondage, promised the peasants freedom from taxes and debts, promised murderers a free life in Palestine and promised all forgiveness for their sins and entrance to life eternal.

"Knights and nobles assembled armed bands of peasants and serfs to march across Europe and free Jerusalem from the infidels. Along the way, they would have to cross the Rhine River where Jewish communities had been established since the glory days of the Roman Empire. As the Crusaders approached these towns, they had a new slogan: 'Kill a Jew and save your soul.'

"Why wait to get to the Holy Land so faraway to kill infidels when so many Jews were nearby? Allow me to tell you what happened in just one German town in the Rhineland," the Prosecutor said as he moved closer to the witness stand.

John leaned forward in the witness chair. "Of course you may tell me Mr. Prosecutor but remember I wasn't there."

"Oh but you were there John. Your Gospel was their inspiration. Let me refresh your memory. This is what you wrote about the Jews in Chapter Eight, Verse 44 of your Gospel: "Ye are of your father, the Devil, and the lusts of your father ye will do." You accused the Jews, all the Jews for all time of being children of the Devil. That is why noble Crusaders could slaughter innocent Jewish children, women and men. Centuries later Christians used bullets and gas instead of swords to kill millions of Jews, those children of the Devil you wrote about."

John jumped from his chair. He turned to the Judge. "Your honor, it's not fair to take my words out of context and blame me for terrible atrocities that happened centuries after I was gone. I admit my language might have been extreme, but my motive was not to kill Jews, but to convert them to the true faith in Jesus Christ, to save their souls for life everlasting.

"It is not fair to judge the New Testament by picking out one sentence and pouncing on it as if that is what the

Bible is about. The New Testament is about Jesus Christ and the example of the love of mankind he showed the world. What if we picked out parts of the Old Testament that told how Joshua would kill everyone in the towns he conquered. Is that how the world should judge the Jews? Is that the message of Moses and the Ten Commandments?"

The Prosecutor approached the bench. "Your honor, John's motives are not on trial here, his words are. His words have been sanctified in the Bible as Gospel Truth. John was declared a Saint and Saint John defamed the Jews, slandered them as children of the Devil and thus deprived them of the right to be treated as sacred human beings. May I continue with the witness your honor?"

"Yes. Yes Mr. Prosecutor. Let's get on with it," the Judge replied in a weary voice.

The Prosecutor returned to face John. "John, on May 26, 1096 Count Emmich led his men into the town of Mainz on the Rhine River. They rampaged through the town searching for Jews. Thousands of Jewish children, women and men were killed."

John again protested to the Judge, "Your honor, that is not what the New Testament is about. Our Bible is about love, love of God, love of Jesus. It is about mercy and brotherhood."

"That is true John," the Prosecutor sighed. "But it is also about hate, hate of the Jews. Let me give you some other examples of Christian love and mercy.

"On July 15, 1205, Pope Innocent III, the most powerful ruler in Europe, issued a proclamation that all Jews were doomed to perpetual servitude and subjugation because they killed Jesus Christ. That was the official doctrine of the Catholic Church for 758 years until finally revoked in 1963 at the Vatican II Conference. Notice that this doctrine of hate was revoked only after the Second World War, after the Holocaust.

"Ten years after condemning Jews to perpetual servitude and subjugation, Pope Innocent III convened the Fourth Lateran Council to plan the Fifth Crusade and to deal with the "Jewish problem." The problem was that the Jews refused to accept Jesus as the true Messiah. There was fear that this only group of non-Christians in all of Europe might lure good Christians away from the faith and thus weaken the Church.

"Among the long list of harsh restrictions adopted by the council was the requirement that all Jews must wear a badge of shame on their clothing. For 500 years, the Jew badge was enforced in most Catholic countries. It finally disappeared in the late 18th Century, the Age of Enlightenment. Adolf Hitler revived the medieval code of the Popes when Jews were forced to wear a yellow Star of David on their coats.

"When the bubonic plague struck Europe in the 14th Century, the people were terrified. A fourth of the population of Europe died in the plague, 25 million people. No one knew what caused the plague or how to cure it. There had to be an explanation. They found one. The Jews did it. The Jews poisoned the wells. After all, they were the children of the Devil. St. John told them so. Tens of thousands of Jews were massacred throughout Europe in the Black Death riots.

"That John is what we saw of the love and mercy brought by your Gospel."

The Judge looked at the large pendulum clock in the back of the courtroom. "We will adjourn now and reconvene tomorrow morning at 10 AM sharp." He banged the gavel down with gusto. The trial was over for day two.

Gerald put the manuscript down. He looked at the large painting over the fireplace. His father, Saul Cohen, smiled at him. The artist captured the mischievous twinkle in his eyes.

"I miss you Dad," Gerald said softly. "You would like this book. I know you would. But how can I do it? It could ruin me. My newspapers, my radio stations, my family. For what? What good would it do?" Saul Cohen smiled at his son, his rich Winnetka son with his Gentile family. What did he know about being a Jew?

Chapter

Eight

LAKE FOREST COLLEGE HAD not been tarnished by the teacher-student scandals that had erupted at the University of Virginia and other campuses. Professors there had used their power to obtain sexual favors from students anxious for higher grades or for the excitement of an affair with an older man. Ben knew several professors were having discreet rendezvous with their students. It was easy to arrange a student conference that might blossom into something more passionate than a discussion of Aristotle. Opportunities were abundant, even at sedate Lake Forest College.

Ben's last appointment for the afternoon was a meeting with Cindy Cunningham to discuss her term paper. Cindy arrived at 5 PM as scheduled. Ben thought they would discuss the Vatican during the Second World War, but Cindy had come to win her hundred dollar bet with Sarah Johnson. She would put St. Benjamin to the test.

After the usual pleasantries, Ben asked: "How's your term paper progressing?"

"It's a bit confusing. Pope John XII has some bitter enemies and some dedicated defenders. I'm not sure who is right."

"The record of the Catholic Church during the Second Word War is still very controversial," Ben replied. "Hitler was a Catholic. Many believed the Pope should have excommunicated him and condemned the Nazi atrocities. Others claim the Pope did not speak out against Hitler because he feared Hitler might close all the churches. Thousands of Jews were saved by very courageous priests and nuns who hid them in convents and churches until the war was over. The wonderful movie *Sound of Music* was true how the nuns in a convent saved the Von Trapp family."

"So which argument do you accept professor?" Cindy asked as she brushed her long blond hair back from her radiant blue eyes.

"Why don't you present both sides of the story Cindy and you decide what real alternatives the Pope had."

"Thanks professor, I'll do that. I know it's late, but may I ask you a personal question?"

"Go ahead. If it's too personal, you may not get an answer."

Cindy pulled her chair up closer to the desk.

"I just finished reading *Naked Truth*. I couldn't believe you wrote it. It is so different from the way you appear in class. I mean those sex scenes are so torrid."

Ben laughed. "I'm afraid that's what sells books these days. You have to toss in a little sex or the readers get bored."

"Well, I thought it was a terrific book. Very suspenseful. In fact, if you don't mind I'd love for you to autograph my copy."

"No problem. Just bring it to class anytime."

"I have it with me." Cindy got up and walked to the table near the door where she had left her briefcase. She took out *Naked Truth* and paused a moment to examine the cover. On the cover, a bare chested man was handcuffed to the bedposts with a nude woman astride him, like a scene from *Basic Instinct*.

Cindy walked around the desk so she would be standing next to Ben. As she opened the book for Ben to sign, Ben could feel her soft breast brush against his shoulder. As Ben signed her book, Cindy raised herself onto his desk. When Ben handed her back her book, Cindy turned the cover to him.

"Did you ever do that?" she asked with a soft laugh.

"Cindy, you certainly are getting personal aren't you?"

"I'll leave whenever you say professor," she pouted.

Ben didn't believe what he heard himself say: "No, I don't mind. To answer your question, I never got into the bondage scene, but I did research it."

"How do you research such a thing?" Cindy asked as she swung her leg back and forth like a sensual metronome.

Ben could feel himself slowly being hypnotized by the steady motion. He forced his eyes away from Cindy's naked thighs and concentrated for a moment on the generous curves pressing against her pink cashmere turtleneck. He quickly sought safety by looking into Cindy's smiling face.

"How do you research such a thing?" Ben repeated the question. "Well, it was a little bizarre. I called a few escort services and told the ladies I would pay for their time, but just wanted to ask them some questions about their work."

"What were the ladies like?" Cindy asked really curious to know.

"They were very attractive women, most of them college graduates. The money was much better than they could make elsewhere. Many thought they were performing a valuable service, like a psychiatrist except their clients got to act out their fantasies."

"So that's how you got all the details for those scenes in your book?"

"That's how Cindy, but it's a trade secret. Let the public think I experimented, it's more enticing."

"Perhaps professor, you should get first-hand experience for your scenes. Why ask questions? Just do it."

Ben was getting uncomfortable. He should put a stop to this silly flirtation. But he was enjoying the repartee with this most attractive young lady. What harm could it do? Just a little conversation.

"I don't think my wife would approve if I went out experimenting on all the devilish scenes I dream up."

"Then experiment on her," Cindy persisted.

"Michelle isn't interested in those bondage scenarios."

"How do you know?"

"I asked her."

"What did she say?"

"She said she thought the whole idea was absurd. That I should keep those ideas in my books and not bring them to bed with me."

"Well, next time you need some research professor, please call me. I'm available."

Cindy hopped off the desk and gathered her things together.

"Good night professor and thank you for your help."

"Good night, Cindy." Her perfume lingered long after she was gone.

Ben was perplexed and amused. Why would Cindy Cunningham throw herself at him?

Cindy was an A student so it couldn't be for a better grade. Maybe she found him attractive. What a flattering thought.

In bed with Michelle that night, Ben made love to his wife.

"Hey tiger, you were terrific tonight," Michelle whispered. "You taking some new vitamin pills?"

"No pills honey. You just inspire me."

"I'm glad. Come back anytime."

"I'll be back for sure."

"Don't forget," Michelle said as she kissed Ben and rolled to her side of their queen size bed.

"Good night," Ben replied, thankful that "Good night Cindy" had not slipped out.

How can you make love to one woman while thinking about another woman? It must be that crazy midlife crisis he heard about.

As Ben drifted off to sleep, he imagined Cindy climbing on his chest. She was holding handcuffs in one hand and a small whip in the other. "Do it Cindy, do it," he fantasized before sleep carried him away from the blue-eyed temptress.

In the middle of the night, on the narrow edge of sleep, Ben's mind was obsessed with a fantasy. He saw Cindy standing next to him while he lay in a strange bed. She was dressed in a black body suit, like Cat Woman. He tried to get up but his wrists were firmly tied to the bedposts with white silk scarves. She smiled her seductive smile and climbed on top of him. She sat on his chest and slowly removed his necktie. Then she carefully unbuttoned his shirt. She reached over to the night table and took a long silver scissors in her hand.

"What are you doing?" Ben cried with alarm in his dream.

"Trust me," Cindy said. She took the scissors and cut open his undershirt. She pulled it back so she could see his bare chest. Cindy moved down his body and undid his belt. She unzipped his pants and pulled them off.

"Stop Cindy!" Ben shouted in his dream.

"Do you really want me to stop professor?"

Ben yanked his arms with all his strength, but the knots held. He could not escape. He was helpless with Cindy on top of him.

"You should stop Cindy," Ben pleaded.

"Why should I stop professor? You do like what I'm doing to you don't you?"

"I shouldn't like it, but I do. I should be home with my wife."

"She'll never know. We won't tell. It will be our secret."

Ben could feel his erection straining against his jockey shorts.

"Do you want me to untie you professor? Tell the truth."

Cindy slid her hand under Ben's shorts and grabbed his penis and stroked it softly.

"Should I untie you professor?"

"No." Ben whispered.

"I didn't hear you," Cat Woman purred.

"No, I said," Ben was about to explode.

"Louder Ben. Say it louder," Cindy demanded.

"No! God no!"

Cindy removed his shorts.

"How do you feel professor?"

"I feel I'm going to explode," Ben panted.

"Not yet professor, not yet."

Cindy reached over to the night table and undid a Trojan. She expertly and gently fitted it on Ben's engorged penis. "Are you ready professor?"

"No Cindy, I can't do it." Ben sobbed. "I can't do it. Please let me go!"

And then Ben woke up.

Chapter

Nine

MICHAEL MORRIS HAD EXHAUSTED his list of contacts. For three weeks he had pitched *The Trial of St. John* to publishers in New York, Boston and Chicago. No one was interested in a book attacking the Bible. No one would even read it. How could he let it die? The world was awash in Jewish blood from centuries of unspeakable crimes. Was no one to blame?

Michael had one last hope. He punched the number on his smartphone.

"Hello." a cheerful female voice answered.

"Hello Sandra. It's Michael Morris."

"Michael, what a pleasant surprise. Now that I'm a retired lady I thought you forgot all about me."

"Don't forget, you're a very rich retired lady," Michael said with a laugh.

"How could I forget? Salesmen call me all day. Everything from tax-free bonds to cemetery lots.

That article in the *Wall Street Journal* about my sale of Harborside Press to Gerald Crane unleashed the horde to my doorstep."

"What do you think about retired life Sandra?"

"It's a bore. I need to keep busy Michael or I'll rust away."

"So what are you going to do?" Michael asked.

"I thought of opening a brothel, but my lawyer advised against it. He's such a pill. Never lets me have any fun."

"I've got a proposition for you Sandra."

"It's about time. I haven't been propositioned for so long that I forgot how to do it."

"Not that kind of proposition you hussy. A business proposition."

"Not a pizza parlor I hope. I just turned that one down yesterday."

"No Sandra. Not pizza, publishing.

"Did you forget Michael? I'm out of publishing."

"You may be out of publishing, but you are still Sandra Price. Everyone in the industry and the media know you. If you get behind a book, they will sit up and take notice."

"You're sweet Michael, but I'm finished with publishing. I have no office, no staff, no authors."

"You can have *The Trial of St. John.*"

"You haven't been able to sell it?"

"No one will touch it," Michael said sadly.

"I don't blame them. It's a killer," Sandra replied.

"Sandra you could do it. You sold Harborside Press. You've got your money. What could you lose?"

"How about my life?"

"Sandra, you want to live forever?"

"Not forever Michael. Just long enough to enjoy my new fortune."

"Sandra, you know Ben's book is important. You're the only one who can save it."

"Michael, the book needs work. It needs a top-notch editor, sophisticated publicity, good production, fast distribution. I'm an old lady. What do you want from me?"

"Don't give me that old lady routine. You're a feisty dame who knows more about this business in your little finger than all those hotshot editors in New York."

"What about my 'no compete' clause with Gerald?"

"You're not competing with him. He's too chicken to handle Ben's book. This will be a one shot deal Sandra. You'll make history."

"Or, I'll be history. Who would be the editor?" Sandra asked.

"The best in the business, you."

"You're really serious aren't you Michael?"

"Never been more serious in my life. With your contacts Sandra, Ben will be on every talk show and write-ups in all the major papers. *The Trial of St. John* will be the hottest book in town."

"It would be fun to do," Sandra said visualizing the excitement of a new book, a very controversial book that the public should have the right to see. "Since I can't live forever, I might as well go out with a bang. OK Michael. I'll do it. What should we call our new company?"

Michael was delighted. Ben's book would be born. Let the public decide if the Gospel of John was responsible for all the anti-Semitism that led to the Holocaust. "How about L'Chaim Publications?"

"Great suggestion," Sandra replied with enthusiasm. "L'Chaim, 'to life'". Send the manuscript back Michael. I'll go to work on it right away." Sandra hung up the phone and felt young again. She wasn't just a rich old lady. She was Sandra Price, the best publisher in the business and she would prove it with *The Trial of St. John*.

The next day Sandra had *The Trial of St. John* in her hands once more. This would be the last book she would ever publish. It would be her swan song to the world of books she loved so much. She would give it her best shot. Sandra settled into her comfortable sitting room and reread the manuscript.

The Trial of St. John

CHAPTER THREE

THE THIRD DAY OF the trial of St. John began precisely at 10 AM. The Romans had a passion for order. The judge would rule his courtroom as he once commanded his legions, with perfect discipline.

"Mr. Prosecutor, are you prepared to proceed?"

"Yes your honor."

"Well, get on with it." The Judge settled back in his chair. He missed the roar of battle. The charging chariots, horsemen with flashing swords. The Empire depended on his wit, his wisdom and his bravery to smash the enemies of Rome. That time had passed, but history recalled his courage. In his lifetime, Rome was master of the world. None could equal the glory of Rome. Napoleon tried. Hitler tried. After a few years, they were gone, their empires in shambles. Rome ruled the world for centuries. There would never be her equal. Let these men fight over words. He had been master of continents.

The Prosecutor walked slowly to the witness stand. John was sitting erect, finely groomed, dignified.

"John, have you reviewed the material I prepared for you?" the Prosecutor asked in his usual soft voice.

"Of course I have," John replied.

The Prosecutor moved closer to the witness. "I'd like to direct your attention to the section on Spain. In the year 1487, Pope Innocent VIII appointed Tomas de Torquemada the Grand Inquisitor. Torquemada was the personal priest for King Ferdinand and Queen Isabella.

"He was a beast," John said vehemently.

"Yes he was John, but he was your beast. You are the one who made the Jews guilty of killing Jesus Christ. You are the one who called the Jews children of the Devil. Why do you think the Jews were hated so much that Christians were given permission to torment and murder Jews throughout the ages? Because the New Testament, especially the Gospel of John, pictured the Jews as a sinful people who deserved to be punished forever.

John protested vigorously. "I never wrote that the Jews should be murdered. Don't blame me for all the horrors that happened to the Jews. I wasn't there. I did not do those terrible things."

"No John, of course you were not there," the Prosecutor continued. "You didn't personally tie thousands of secret Jews to the stake and burn them alive. But your words were there. Every day for centuries, even today in the 21st Century, good Christians study the Bible and learn to hate the Jews. Is it any wonder that Jews have been murdered, millions of them?

"If you want to read the gory details about the horrors Torquemada inflicted on the secret Jews in Spain, I suggest you read Chaim Potok's book *Wanderings*."

"I don't need to read about Torquemada," John replied forcefully. "I know all about him. The man was insane. He should have been stopped," John said with genuine feeling.

"Who could stop him John?" the Prosecutor demanded. "He was appointed by the Pope. The King and Queen of Spain were his friends and admirers. Torquemada wasn't satisfied with burning thousands of Jews alive at the stake. He persuaded King Ferdinand and Queen Isabella to make Spain a pure Catholic country, expel every Jew and Muslim from Spanish soil.

"The Jews had lived in Spain for 1500 years. Under Muslim (Moor) rule, the Jews flourished in the 8th and 9th centuries and helped make Spain the most advanced, civilized nation in Europe. The 'Golden Age' of Judaism in philosophy, literature, art, government, medicine was in Muslim Spain.

"On March 31, 1492 the year Columbus discovered America, the Jews of Spain discovered they had no home. On that date, the King and Queen of Spain signed the edict of expulsion. Jews who converted to Catholicism could stay. Those who refused to convert had to leave the country within four months. The Jews were forbidden to take any gold, silver or diamonds with them.

"Abram Leon Sachar in his book, *A History of the Jews,* estimates that up to 800,000 Jews were expelled from Spain, Portugal and Sicily during the Inquisition.

"Fortunately, the Muslim Ottoman Empire opened its doors to the Jews. Tens of thousands of Jews found refuge in Turkey and North Africa. European countries, except for Italy and Holland, slammed the door shut on Jewish refugees."

"Those were certainly terrible times," John said, shifting uncomfortably in the witness chair. "But the Jews didn't have to die, they didn't have to leave Spain. Why didn't they just convert and save their lives and their homes?"

"Thousands did convert John. I'm sure there is Jewish blood in many Spanish veins. The Jews are a stubborn people. When it comes to their God, they can be absolutely obstinate. They refused to renounce their God. The Jews really believed there was a God, the same God who talked to Moses and gave us the Ten Commandments.

"Your Christians refused to renounce Jesus and pray to the Roman gods. Instead, they chose to face the lions in the Coliseum. Likewise, the Jews died for their religion or fled Spain as paupers."

Sandra put the manuscript down. How many Jews would die at the stake for their God today, she wondered. For America, yes. For Israel, yes. But for God, probably not. And how many Christians would be willing to face the hungry lions and cheering Romans rather than forsake Jesus. Not very many, she thought. Sandra reopened the manuscript. She would finish the third day of the trial of St. John.

The Judge leaned forward. "Let's move on, Mr. Prosecutor."

"Of course, your honor. John, in the notes I gave you, there is a section on the corruption of the Church in the Middle Ages."

"I read it. Absolutely disgraceful conduct. I would never have permitted such scandals."

"I'm sure you would not," the Prosecutor agreed. There is a famous quote from Lord Acton which certainly applies to the Catholic Church in the 16th Century. He wrote:

'Power corrupts. Absolute power corrupts absolutely.'

"The priests then were not only corrupt, they were terribly greedy. Priests would sell indulgences to the peasants which would save their souls from hell for the sins they had committed.

"One priest, Martin Luther, finally rebelled. Luther was a professor of theology at the University of Wittenberg, Germany. On October 31, 1517, Luther nailed his 95 protests on the door of the All Saints Church in Wittenberg and thus began the Reformation.

"Martin Luther denounced the selling of indulgences, but he did not denounce the Bible. Luther accepted your Gospel as sacred writing. You said the Jews were children of the Devil. Martin Luther believed you as did all good Christians. Michelangelo's exquisite sculpture of Moses shows horns coming out of the head of Moses to show him as a child of the Devil.

"Martin Luther wrote a pamphlet titled: "Concerning the Jews and Their Lies". Adolf Hitler praised the writings of Luther for their vicious attacks on the Jews. No wonder that the German people cooperated with the Nazis. They had been conditioned for centuries to hate Jews."

The Prosecutor walked to his table and picked up a small pamphlet. He walked slowly to the witness and showed him the pamphlet. "John let me read you some of what the founder of the Protestant religion said that Christians should do to the Jews."

After reading several pages, the Prosecutor was interrupted by a shout from the bench.

"Enough! Enough already." The Judge tried to maintain his imperial dignity, but the outrageous language of Martin Luther was too much. The Judge wondered how such a courageous, intelligent leader like Martin Luther could advocate such cruelty. The Judge banged the gavel down harshly.

"Tomorrow, 10 AM sharp."

The Judge gathered his purple robe and stormed out of the courtroom.

Sandra closed the book. *The Trial of St. John* could ignite a storm of protests. Could Christians disown the Gospel of John? What about Martin Luther? The Founder of Protestantism, a rabid anti-Semite. How could Christians revere such a man?

What might some fanatic Christians do to the author and publisher of a book that places blame for centuries of massacres of the Jews on the Holy Bible? Sandra Price would publish *The Trial of St. John*, but she had to admit that for the first time in her life she was really frightened.

Chapter

Ten

BEN PICKED UP HIS school mail and went to his office to scan the usual assortment of notices and letters. This morning there was a small box in the mail. There was no return address. Ben opened the box carefully. Inside, wrapped in pink tissue paper were two sets of handcuffs. The note read: "Dear Professor, for your research. Call me anytime. Cindy." Cindy's phone number and address were on the bottom of the note.

Ben picked up one set of handcuffs. They were heavy steel, not toys. A person in these cuffs would be helpless, completely at the mercy of whoever held the key. The thought excited Ben. The thought of Cindy possessing him, forcing herself on him was from fantasyland. Except it could really happen. All he had to do was call.

Ben mused at his reaction. How could he even think of such a thing? Cindy was just a 20 year-old-girl, a very enticing young lady to be sure, but trouble with a capital

T. He was ashamed he would even consider making such a call. He loved his wife, he adored his daughter. He didn't need any extracurricular activity to be perfectly happy. And yet, some *Basic Instinct* urged him to explore a new dimension in his life. To break free of his routine world of teaching and writing and being the perfect mate, the perfect Dad.

Why shouldn't he do a little research for his next novel? How could he really describe the irresistible sexual urges of his characters if he continued to suppress his own deep sexual desires? What harm would it do? It would be a secret hour. One lousy little hour out of a lifetime of impeccable behavior.

"You damn fool Ben Sanders," he said to himself. "Don't you dare make that call."

What was it about women that drove men to do such stupid things he wondered? Important men, powerful men had ruined their reputations because of some passionate affair with a tempting woman. President Bill Clinton and his sexual games with Monica Lewinsky in the Oval Office came to mind.

Ben Sanders would not be that dumb. He would not betray everything he loved and treasured for the thrill of an orgasm. Still, there was that primal ache that defied reason, that drove men to do what they surely knew they should not do.

Of course, Ben could rationalize it. An evening with Cindy would be for scientific research. He was gathering insights for his next book. What if he allowed himself to be handcuffed just to see what it felt like? Then it would be up to Cindy. If she took advantage of his helpless position, the guilt would be hers. He would be the innocent victim. Can you be a victim if you plan the crime?

Ben was ashamed of himself for wanting to make that call, for wanting to feel a vibrant young woman devour him with her boundless energy. Ben carefully placed the handcuffs back in the box and put the box in his bottom drawer behind a stack of files.

"Enough fantasizing," he said to himself. "Back to the wonderful world of normalcy and routine."

Ben was secretly proud of himself. He had stuffed the genie of erotic passion back into the bottle. He was safe, for now, from the temptation to do something really stupid.

When Ben arrived home, he was disappointed Jenny was not there to greet him with her usual big "Daddy hug." He wanted to hold his daughter and his wife and tell them, oh so truly, how very much he loved them. He would erase the sin of even thinking about Cindy by folding Jenny and Michelle in his arms and holding them forever.

"Hi Honey," Michelle called from the kitchen. "Jenny with you?"

"No. I thought she would be home by now."

Michelle tried to think why Jenny was not home yet. She gave her husband a quick hug.

"She had a *Cinderella* rehearsal after school. I guess it went longer than expected."

"I'll drive by the school and give her a ride. It will be dark soon and I don't want Jenny walking home alone."

"Good idea Ben. Dinner's almost ready so come right home."

The door to Lincoln Junior High School was locked. Ben rang the bell. In a few minutes, he saw a teacher's face in the wired glass. She opened the door.

"I'm Ben Sanders, Jenny's father."

"I remember you from our open house Mr. Sanders. I'm Doris Thomas, Jenny's drama teacher. Jenny is terrific. She is a perfect *Cinderella*."

"I came to give her a ride home."

"Jenny's not here. Rehearsal was over an hour ago. Maybe she stopped at a friend's house."

"Probably so. Thank you, Mrs. Thomas."

Ben drove home with a knot in his stomach. That was not like Jenny. She always called if she went to a friend's house. Not to worry, he assured himself. This was Highland Park with its lush green lawns, towering trees and expensive homes. That terrible incident a year ago at St. Catherine's was a rare case, a fading memory.

Michelle was waiting at the door.

"Where is she?" Michelle demanded when she saw Ben get out of the car without Jenny.

"Mrs. Thomas said rehearsal was over an hour ago. She's probably at a friend's house."

"Jenny always calls," Michelle insisted.

"I know," Ben said trying to disguise his worry.

"I'll call her friends," Michelle said as she pulled out her smartphone.

Michelle made six quick phone calls. Jenny was not with any of her friends.

"Ben, I did get some information from Leah Jacobs. Leah said Jenny walked her home, but did not come in the house. Before she closed the door, Leah said she saw Jenny talking to a lady delivering flowers next door. Ben, I'm scared. Where could she be?"

"It's too soon to worry. I'm sure she will call soon."

Ben was right. At 7 p.m. the phone rang.

"Hi Daddy. It's Jenny."

"I know. Where are you? Mom and I have been worried sick."

"I'm OK. A man and a woman took me away in a delivery van. They didn't hurt me. They said they just wanted to talk to you."

A husky voice came on the phone.

"Mr. Sanders, my name is Karl. Your daughter is safe and no harm will come to her. I just took her so you would pay close attention to what I am going to tell you."

"I'm listening."

"My friends and I know about the book you wrote. We know you are slandering our Bible. That has us very upset. If you don't want Jenny hurt, don't print that book. And don't call the police. I'll know if you do. I'll call you tomorrow." The phone clicked off.

Michelle could tell from Ben's face that something terrible had happened.

"Jenny's been kidnapped," Ben said in stunned disbelief.

"Oh, my God! What can we do?" Michelle sobbed.

"I don't know. The man warned me not to call the police."

Ben held his wife. Her tears wet his cheeks.

"We can't just sit here," Michelle cried.

"I'll call Michael," Ben said. "Maybe he will have some ideas."

Michael Morris couldn't believe it. How could anyone grab a young girl off the street in Highland Park? Not for money, but to keep *The Trial of St. John* off the market. Censorship by terror in America. Michael advised Ben to do nothing. Just wait for the next call.

Michael called Sandra Price.

"I was afraid the 'crazies' would react," Sandra said after hearing Michael's story. I thought Ben and I might get some threats, but it is so awful to take their hate out on a child. Of course, I'll hold up printing the book until Jenny is home safe and sound."

"Sandra, do you have any contacts with the FBI?"

"I don't," Sandra replied, "but I know who does."

"Who?"

"Gerald Crane. He knows everybody."

"Please call him Sandra. We need a top level contact so this doesn't come out. There are Christians everywhere you know," Michael said with a weak laugh.

It was after 8 p.m. when Gerald Crane received the call from Sandra. He was annoyed. His home was his sanctuary. He definitely did not like business calls to his home in the evening. His attitude changed completely when he heard the story of the kidnapping of Jenny Sanders.

"I do know the head of the FBI in Chicago, Vincent Conrad, an excellent man. I'll call him at home and get his advice. Sit tight Sandra. I'll call you right back."

Vincent Conrad advised the chairman of the Chicago Media Group to have Ben Sanders call him at home immediately. They would devise a plan that would only involve the FBI, not the local police.

Ben called Vincent Conrad and agreed to have two FBI agents come to the house in the morning with special telephone monitoring equipment. They would come in a van marked North Shore Plumbing.

It was a tearful night for Ben and Michelle. Ben kept repeating over and over: "I'm so sorry Michelle. I never thought anyone would harm Jenny. God, I'll never forgive myself if they hurt her."

"They promised they wouldn't hurt her Ben. Just forget your damn book."

"Of course I'll drop it. Nothing in this world is more important than Jenny."

They wept together and held one another in the darkness. Nothing mattered now except Jenny. Money, fame, their beautiful home – all worthless without their daughter. Sleep finally conquered their pain. The tears stopped, until tomorrow.

Chapter

Eleven

JENNY SURVEYED HER SURROUNDINGS. She was in a basement, a nicely furnished basement with knotty pine walls, a washroom, TV, bookcase and a bed. There was no door to the outside, just a staircase to the main floor. The door was locked. She tried it already. There were two windows in her room. Each window was covered with a heavy plywood panel. Before Karl nailed the plywood over the window frames, he showed Jenny that there were iron burglar bars on each window. No one could get in. There was no way for Jenny to get out.

Jenny felt so stupid for getting into the delivery van, but it seemed harmless at the time. After she left Leah, she saw a lady in a delivery uniform carrying a large floral arrangement. The lady called to Jenny.

"Excuse me. Can you help me?"

'I'll try," Jenny had replied.

The lady came close to Jenny and showed her the address card. "The boss gave me the wrong address. I have flowers for a Mrs. Ben Sanders. Would you know where the Sanders' house is?"

"That's easy. That's my house." Jenny knew her Dad liked to surprise them both with unexpected gifts. He hadn't sent flowers in a long time.

"Could you hop in and show me the house so I don't go to the wrong place again?"

Jenny readily agreed. The lady seemed nice and she was very pretty. Certainly no thought of danger entered her mind. Once Jenny was in the van, the lady started the engine and drove down Burton Street toward the Sanders home. After the first block, Jenny was startled to hear a man's voice behind her.

"Don't be frightened Jenny." She felt a powerful hand grab her wrist.

"Don't scream or I'll have to hurt you," he warned.

The lady assured Jenny they would not hurt her if she kept quiet and did what she was told. Jenny was scared, but there was no way to escape. She climbed into the back of the van and laid down on a mattress on the floor. Karl sat in the seat next to the mattress. From the floor, Jenny couldn't see where they were going. The van made so many turns that Jenny lost all sense of direction.

They drove for a few hours until it was dark. Then the lady, Karl called Kitty, handed Jenny a cell phone to call home. Jenny wanted to cry when she heard her Dad's voice, but struggled to control herself so her parents wouldn't be even more worried. After the call, they drove for another two hours.

When Jenny was let out of the van, she saw she was inside a two car garage attached to the house. The garage door was closed behind her so no one had seen her get out of the van. Kitty stayed in the van while the man took Jenny inside the house. Jenny never saw Kitty again.

Inside the house, Karl introduced Jenny to his wife Nicole. Nicole seemed very nice and motherly. Jenny was taken directly to the basement rec room. Nicole brought her a chicken dinner with all the trimmings and showed her how to work the TV. Nicole assured Jenny that no one was going to hurt her. She was just going to be their guest for a few days while they convinced her father not to publish *The Trial of St. John* because it insulted their Bible.

Jenny was angry that she had been kidnapped, but she was no longer frightened. No one had hurt her and Karl and Nicole seemed like a nice middle age couple with quite a lovely home. Jenny knew her parents would do anything to get her back. Jenny watched TV for a while then crawled into bed. She slept soundly through the night.

Karl called at noon the next day. Ben had stayed home to comfort Michelle. He certainly couldn't face a class until his daughter was safely home again. Ben heard the same husky voice:

"This is Karl."

"Karl, I must speak to Jenny before you go any further. I have to know she is Okay."

"Just a moment. I'll get her."

"Hi Daddy. I'm fine. No one has hurt me or anything. I just want to come home."

"Darling, are you sure you are all right?" Michelle was on the extension.

"I'm fine Mom. They are really a nice couple. They just don't like Daddy's book about the Bible."

Ben and Michelle could tell from Jenny's voice that she was indeed Okay. The two FBI agents were recording the call. They couldn't trace the call because it came from a 'burner' cell phone.

"Mr. Sanders," Karl was back. "Get a pencil and write this down"

"I'm ready."

"This story is to appear in tomorrow's *Chicago Tribune:* 'Professor Benjamin Sanders announced today that the publication of his book, *The Trial of St. John*, a fictional story about the New Testament has been permanently cancelled because of errors discovered in the text.' As soon as we see the story in the *Tribune*, Jenny can go home."

"'I'll cancel the book. Just don't hurt Jenny," Ben pleaded.

"We won't hurt her Mr. Sanders. You keep your end of the deal and we'll keep ours. One more thing. When Jenny is home, don't try to print your book. We know where you live. We know where Jenny is every day. If your book ever appears in the bookstores, your little girl will be dead. I couldn't do it myself, but others in our group would certainly kill her. You understand."

"I understand. The story will be in the *Tribune* tomorrow."

"One last thing, Mr. Sanders. I know you did not call the police. I have sources everywhere." The phone clicked off.

The story appeared the next day in a small box on the front page of the *Tribune*. Gerald Crane had arranged it with the *Tribune* publisher. Ben and Michelle waited anxiously all morning. Finally, just after 1 PM the phone rang.

"Hi Daddy. Come and get your Cinderella girl."

Ben and Michelle ran to the car to pick up Jenny at her school. The two FBI agents followed in their car. Jenny was standing by the main entrance. The Sanders family was reunited with hugs and kisses and tears. The FBI agents followed them home and then spent two hours debriefing Jenny and recording everything she could remember about the kidnappers and the three days she spent as their "guest."

Chapter

Twelve

THE 27TH DAY IN the month of Nissan in the Hebrew calendar is the holiday of Yom Ha Shoah, a day of Remembrance for the six million Jews killed in the Holocaust. Ben and Michelle went to the Memorial Service at Beth El Synagogue in Highland Park. It was a cool April evening and the early spring leaves were still visible in the sun's dying palette of reds and oranges that painted the western sky.

As they entered the large auditorium, they were motioned up to the bimah. There were four long tables covered with small squat glasses. Each glass had a candle embedded in wax. Ben and Michelle followed the line of worshippers up to the tables. Each was handed a lighted candle and lit one of the memorial Yahrzeit candles and then walked off the bimah and took a seat. The auditorium was dim. The congregation silent. The candles flickered their message of sadness and horror.

The Chassan chanted "Ani Ma'amin" ("I Believe") with tears in his voice. This was the prayer chanted by the devout as they were marched into the gas chambers at Auschwitz. When all the candles had been lit and every seat filled, the Rabbi walked to the pulpit.

With his clerical robe, kippah and tallit, the Rabbi carried with him the tradition of over 5700 years of the Jewish people. Rabbi Arnold Feinstein had been born after the Holocaust. To him, it was history, unbelievable in its cruelty and scope, but history to him. His dark mustache and trimmed beard softened his angular face and made him look older than he was. His small beard was a compromise between the wild, untamed beards of the orthodox and the clean-shaven Reform Jews.

After leading the congregation through the prayers, the Rabbi introduced the guest speaker: "We are all privileged to have as our speaker this evening a member of our congregation and a survivor of Auschwitz. As many of you know, Max Levi arrived in America after the war as a young man without money, without family, without friends. By his genius and very hard work, Max built one of the largest retail chains in the United States. It is my great pleasure and honor to introduce our friend, Mr. Max Levi."

Max Levi strode to the pulpit quickly. He looked more like a retired football coach than the proprietor of 300 ladies apparel shops. He was 74 years old, six foot three inches tall, broad shoulders, trim body, bald except for a fringe of snow white hair that circled his head. He had dark brown eyes, a prominent nose and thin lips. He rarely smiled and always worked.

Max spoke perfect English with only a slight trace of a Hungarian accent. He spoke in a deep bass voice: "What can I tell you about the Holocaust that you do not already know? The libraries are filled with books about the Holocaust. Memoirs of the survivors, histories by the scholars, excuses by those who helped the Nazis kill Jews.

"It's all there. You can read about Auschwitz, Buchenwald, Sobibor, Chelmno, Bergen-Belsen, Treblinka, Dachau. You will not believe what you read. But it is true. I saw it. I smelled it. I lived it.

"There are endless stories of horror, but I will spare you the details. Some would have you believe that the Jews were guilty of their own massacre. That they went like sheep to the slaughter. That resistance like the courageous, hopeless Warsaw Ghetto uprising were too few. Do not judge if you were not there. Do not condemn the sick, half-starved slaves for not charging the Nazi machine guns.

"According to Raul Hilberg, author of *The Destruction of the European Jews* which was the prime source for the movie *Shoah*, 500,000 Jews, mostly Hungarians, were killed at Auschwitz between May and November 1944. During that same time, bombers from the United States 15th Air Force in Italy were bombing industrial targets only a few miles from the gas chambers. Jewish leaders urgently appealed to the British and American governments to bomb the gas chambers and the rail lines leading to Auschwitz. The request was denied. They were told it would interfere with the war effort.

"I wonder if 3,000 American or British citizens were being sent into the gas chambers every single day, if a few bombs might have been diverted from the war effort?

"Do you want to find guilt? Look for the murderers, not the victims. Look for our "friends" who closed their borders and closed their eyes. Yom Ha Shoah is not for the dead. It is for us the living. To burn into our memories the deliberate murder of six million Jews. Six million children, women and men. Six million dreams. Do not forget them. Do not allow your children to forget them. Do not allow the world to forget them."

Max Levi left the pulpit. The Rabbi came forward to give the closing benediction and the Cantor led the congregation in the singing of "Hatikvah" ("The Hope"), the national anthem of the State of Israel. At least now Jews had a home where they would always be welcome.

After services, Ben and Michelle joined the group in front of the pulpit to greet the Rabbi and congratulate Max Levi on his very moving talk.

"Mr. Levi, thank you for sharing your thoughts with us tonight," Michelle said.

"I'm glad I could come," Max replied.

"I'm Michelle Sanders and this is my husband Ben."

"I'm very pleased to meet you both," Max smiled.

Michelle had more in mind that just a social hello. Her husband was the author in the family, but she was the saleslady. What good was Ben's book if it was never published? Perhaps Max Levi, multi-millionaire Max Levi, might have a suggestion for them.

"Mr. Levi, may I send you a copy of Ben's manuscript about the roots of the Holocaust?"

"I'd be pleased to read it," Max said cordially. "What's the title?"

"The Trial of St. John. I'd be very interested in your comments," Ben replied.

"Well, nice meeting you both." Max shook hands with Ben and Michelle and slowly made his way out of the synagogue. The Yom Ha Shoah service was over. But for Max Levi, Yom Ha Shoah would never be over. The nightmare of Auschwitz clung to him every day like a menacing shadow. He survived. The world must never forget those who did not.

Chapter

Thirteen

"This is definitely your house," Michelle Sanders said as she glided her Lincoln Continental to a smooth stop in front of 661 Terrace Lane. She stepped out of the car and felt the chill breeze from Lake Michigan. Her client, Howard Edward Greenfield, one of Chicago's hotshot commodity traders, joined her in front of the car.

"Looks nice," Howard admitted. "Might have possibilities."

"Does it ever!" Michelle's enthusiasm was genuine. This was her own listing, the biggest she ever had and it was a fantastic house. It was set on a high bluff overlooking the lake in the posh North Shore suburb of Glencoe.

"Let me show you the grounds first." Michelle had an instinct for the dramatic. She was setting the stage for her six million dollar sales pitch. First, they walked over to the glass domed swimming pool.

"Is this gorgeous, or is this gorgeous?" The 60 foot swimming pool was surrounded by green indoor-outdoor carpeting with white lounge chairs and tables neatly arranged on both sides of the pool. A red telephone was conspicuous on each side of the pool. In the far corner was a Jacuzzi with another red telephone mounted nearby.

"Now watch this," Michelle opened a panel on the wall near the Jacuzzi. She pushed a button. The glass ceiling dome slid open and the cool April air enveloped them.

"Howard this is fantasyland." Michelle squeezed his arm instinctively. Howard smiled at her. Michelle blushed and removed her hand quickly. Her own fantasy had unprofessionally moved her too close to one of Chicago's most eligible bachelors.

"Let me show you the tennis courts and the lake view," Michelle said, slipping smoothly back into her role as the star saleslady for the Glencoe Real Estate Company. They walked across the lawn, past the tennis courts to the edge of the bluff. Michelle felt like a teenager on her first date. "This is crazy," she said to herself. "I'm a happily married woman and I have no business thinking about Howard Edward Greenfield, his wavy black hair, his athletic slim build, his soft grey eyes." Michelle gave herself a mental kick in the behind. "Let's get down to business," she said to herself sternly. "Howard, can I show you the house now?"

"It's so lovely here," Howard replied, ignoring her question.

"It really is," Michelle agreed. "May I ask you a personal question? You know we have to qualify our clients to be sure they can afford the type of properties we are showing. I really should have gone into this at the office, but your reputation preceded you. Still, a six million dollar investment is a lot of money."

"I can afford it," Howard replied with a smile.

"Would you like me to tell you what the monthly payments would be on a house like this? Michelle whipped out her trusty mortgage calculator from her purse and started figuring.

"Let me see, with 20% down, that's $1,200,000, you need a mortgage of $4,800,000. Now that would mean a monthly payment of ...."

"I won't need a mortgage," Howard interrupted her.

"You won't need a mortgage?" Michelle repeated dumbly. My God, she thought, this guy is 35-years-old and he's got six million dollars in cash! "You won't need a mortgage," Michelle repeated once again.

Howard laughed.

God, he's even got a great laugh, Michelle thought. "Don't you want the interest deduction?" Michelle persisted.

"I'd rather have the worry deduction," Howard said. "You see, the commodity business is a very tricky business. You can make a lot of money. I mean really big money very fast. But, you can lose it all just as fast. Right now, I have quite a bit of cash. I want to park it somewhere in a safe place where I can't get my hands on it instantly. My new home will be my security blanket. All paid for. Nothing to worry about."

"Sounds wonderful," Michelle said sincerely.

"Howard, can I ask you why you want such a big house? I understand from office gossip that you're a bachelor?"

"You understand right Michelle. But, I have a lot of friends. I need a big investment, so why not a big house?"

"Of course, why not?" Michelle happily agreed.

"Well, shall we go inside and see if this is the one?"

"No thank you, Michelle," Howard replied with his winning smile.

"No?" Michelle repeated in amazement. "You don't want to see this fantastic house?"

"That's right. I don't want to see it," Howard replied, still smiling.

Michelle was crushed. Stupid girl, she thought. Thinking this hotshot millionaire was going to be a pushover.

"Michelle, don't look so disappointed," Howard said with a laugh.

"I'm sorry. That's very unprofessional of me. I was just so sure you would like this house. It's really the best home on the North Shore in this price range."

"I believe you Michelle. I do like this house."

"You do like it, but you don't want to see it?"

"That's right. I do like it and I don't want to see it. I want to buy it."

"'You want to buy this house, but you don't want to see the inside of it? Howard, you're rich and you're famous, but Howard my friend, you're crazy! No one, absolutely no one, ever bought a six million dollar house without seeing it."

"I just did," Howard said with his infectious laugh.

"But how can you do that?" Michelle just couldn't understand why Howard would spend so much money and not even see what he was buying. "Maybe the sinks are all stuffed, the plaster peeling, the carpets a hideous orange," Michelle protested.

"You tell me Michelle. Are the sinks stuffed up, the plaster peeling, the carpets a hideous color?"

"God no! The house is perfect. A real gem. Picture windows overlooking the lake, a fabulous kitchen, Roman baths, marble reception hall. It's just beautiful."

"I thought it would be," Howard laughed again.

"But Howard, are you really going to spend six million dollars without even looking at the house?" Michelle asked in amazement. "Why in the world would you do that?"

"For the fun of it. To see the startled look on your face. Look, I spent six million dollars this morning on pork belly contracts. Have you ever seen a pork belly?"

"No. I never saw a pork belly, and I have absolutely no idea why you would want to buy six million dollars of them."

"Well, I've never seen a pork belly either and right now I'm the pork belly King of Chicago," Howard said with his hearty laugh. "So you see, if I can buy pork bellies without examining them, I guess I can buy a house without checking the plumbing. It's no big deal."

"Right. It's no big deal," Michelle eagerly agreed. But it was a very big deal for Michelle and she decided to get it all in writing before the market for pork bellies collapsed.

Fourteen

THE REVEREND PAUL HENRY Porter was a big man. Not just his muscular six foot frame, but his influence, his ability to sway the millions of Americans who listened to his regular Sunday morning sermons from the Gospel Church of Memphis, Tennessee.

He had come a long way from the hell of Vietnam. When he lay dying in the mud, he prayed to a God he had never believed in to save him. He was too young to die. Just twenty-two years old, fresh out of Memphis State College, eager to help America fight communism.

Paul had enlisted in the Marines. Fighting communism was a terrible job. Killing people, destroying villages. There had to be a better way. Before he could find that better way, he was hit in the chest by a sniper bullet. He felt the blood spurt out, his life slowly drain away. There was nothing he could do but pray. And pray he did. Some said Sergeant Alvin Campbell, the black truck driver from

Chicago, saved his life. Paul Henry Porter knew God had sent him. Now he was doing God's work as he had promised when he lay dying in the mud.

His book-lined study was in the school building adjoining the Gospel Church. It had the smell of affluence. The polished mahogany desk, the plush white leather couches and chairs. On the wall were the Reverend's certificates of study and courage. The graduation diplomas from Memphis State College and Yale Divinity School and the Purple Heart and Combat Infantry Badge from the Marine Corps.

The intercom buzzed. Patricia Lee, his secretary since he became pastor of the Gospel Church 15 years ago announced: "Mr. and Mrs. Wilbur Thompson are here Reverend."

"Fine. Show them right in." The Thompsons were from Indianapolis. Generous contributors. Miss Lee had checked the files when they called for an appointment last week. Ten thousand dollars for Reverend Porter's "Fight the Devil" crusade. Of course, he would give them an appointment.

Paul walked to the door to greet the Thompsons. Mrs. Thompson was a petite lady, deep blue eyes, short blonde hair, easy smile. Mr. Thompson was a husky man, as tall as the Reverend with a determined square face. He owned five car dealerships in Indiana and was instrumental in the Indiana law forbidding car sales on Sundays to match the law in neighboring Illinois.

The Reverend did not know the purpose of their visit. Later, he would regret finding out. After the pleasantries, Mr. Thompson got to the point.

"Reverend, can this conversation be privileged, confidential like that with a priest or a lawyer?"

"Yes. By law, I do not have to divulge any confidences given to me as a minister."

"Will you give us your word that what we tell you today will be kept as a solemn secret?"

"Why is it important for me to know this secret?" the Reverend asked.

"It will help you in your 'Fight the Devil' crusade. That's why we drove down from Indianapolis. We believe in your work. I'm sure you know we have made generous contributions to your Church and to your various crusades."

"I do know about your generous gifts and I am very grateful for your support," the Reverend replied.

"I do need your promise of total secrecy before I begin," Wilbur Thompson persisted.

Martha Thompson leaned forward. "Reverend Porter, your sermons really inspire us. We do know the Devil is in this world. We are doing our best to fight Him. We have taken Jesus into our hearts. We are your soldiers in the fight against sin. Our story is important to you Reverend, but it must be our secret, just the three of us."

Martha was so sincere, a true believer. How could Reverend Paul turn them down? What terrible secret did they need to share?

"You have my promise. What you tell me today will never leave this room."

Wilbur Thompson spoke in a steady, firm voice as if he were testifying in a court of law.

"I am the national chairman of a group called the Christian Alliance. We try to instill Christian virtues in our schools and public life by warning our members of threats to our Christian way of life. A few weeks ago, the head of our Chicago chapter, Neville Gardner, called me with very distressing news. A member of his group, Gladys Wright, is the office manager of a Chicago printer. They had just received an order to print 10,000 copies of a book called *The Trial of St. John*.

"Gladys read the galleys and she was horrified. She had keys to the office so she went in one night and made a Xerox copy of the book for Neville. Neville sent the book to me via Federal Express the next day. Martha and I both read the book. It is blasphemous."

Wilbur stopped to catch his breath. Martha took up the story. "We are not violent people Reverend Paul. We never hurt a soul in our lives."

Paul Henry Porter felt his heart tighten. "Please dear God," he said to himself, "don't let this nice couple tell me they killed someone to do Your work on Earth. I did enough of that in Vietnam. What good did all that killing do?"

Martha continued: "*The Trial of St. John* had to be stopped. It blamed the Gospels for all the massacres of the Jews from the Crusades to Auschwitz. What terrible nerve of that professor. He doesn't understand Jesus and the love Christianity has brought into this world."

Wilbur Thompson told Reverend Paul how he and a lady business friend kidnapped Jenny Sanders and brought the young girl to the Thompson home in Indianapolis.

"Jenny was never hurt, not a scratch. Martha cooked for her and made sure she was perfectly comfortable all the time she was a guest in our home. Professor Sanders agreed not to publish *The Trial of St. John* and we took Jenny back home."

The Reverend was silent for a few minutes absorbing what the Thompson's had told him. He leaned forward and looked at Mr. and Mrs. Thompson, good Christians, great contributors and now federal criminals.

"You know what you did was a very serious federal crime," Reverend Paul said.

"We do know," Martha replied quietly. "But it was the only way to stop that terrible book and all the lies about the Gospels."

Wilbur added: "It was the perfect crime. No one will ever know it was us. We both wore disguises. I had a beard, mustache and dark glasses. Martha wore a long black wig and even changed her eye color to dark brown with contact lenses."

"And we used fake names," Martha chimed in. "I was Nicole and Wilbur was Karl."

"The van can't be traced to us," Wilbur continued, "and Jenny had no idea where she was. She was lying down in the back of the van. She never saw the outside of our home. We pulled right into our attached garage."

Wilbur stood up and paced a few moments.

"It really was the perfect crime Reverend. No one got hurt. No one will ever be caught and now no one will ever read those lies about the New Testament."

"Why did you want me to know about this?" Reverend Paul was truly puzzled why they dragged him into their secret.

"We stopped the book Reverend, but we cannot stop the lies," Wilbur replied.

"Professor Sanders is still teaching those lies to his students. They don't understand that if you destroy the Bible there is nothing left but anarchy. We brought you a copy of *The Trial of St. John*. We thought you could fight the professor's ideas in some of your sermons."

Wilbur handed Revered Paul a thick envelope with the Xerox pages of Ben's book.

"Thank you for bringing this to my attention. I'll see what I can do."

The Reverend shook hands with the Thompsons and ushered them to the door. The Thompsons were gone, but now Paul Henry Porter knew the identity of the kidnappers of a young Jewish girl, kidnappers wanted by the FBI.

Chapter

Fifteen

Reverend Porter drove home with a heavy heart. Why do good people do evil things? The Thompsons were a fine, generous churchgoing couple. How could they kidnap a young girl and be proud of themselves for helping Jesus? Perhaps, he was to blame. He urged his listeners to fight sin, to fight the Devil that lurks within all of us. But he wanted them to fight with good deeds, with noble actions, with loving care for the sick and the poor.

Like so many things in his life, the Thompsons reminded him of Vietnam. America only wanted to do good, but what good did all that killing do? Those names engraved on the black wall in Washington, D.C., some were his friends, young men full of life, full of dreams. Why did they die? What for?

Paul drove up the circular drive to the white colonial high on a bluff overlooking the Mississippi River. It was a grand home, a symbol of his success. Only Katherine Anne to share it with him now. Life was moving too fast. His son and daughter had found wonderful mates and moved away.

"You look tired dear," Katherine Anne said softly as she sat beside Paul on the couch after dinner. They watched quietly as the sun painted a blazing farewell across the horizon.

After the glowing sun made its dramatic exit, Paul replied: "Just one of those tough days."

"Want to talk about it?"

"I really can't. Private stuff from one of our big contributors."

"I understand."

Paul knew she really did understand. So much gossip in town. Katherine Anne would rather not know. Then she wouldn't be lying when the women at the club pressed her for all the delicious tidbits.

"I have some work to do tonight dear. I'll be in the study for a few hours."

Paul kissed her gently on the lips and picked up the package the Thompsons had left him.

Katherine Anne went upstairs to their spacious bedroom. Instead of watching TV tonight, she took out of her knitting bag that trashy book the girls at the club were all talking about. She felt guilty about the lurid cover and tore it into tiny pieces and tossed the scraps of paper into the wastebasket. She settled into bed with a sedate blue cloth cover over the *Naked Truth*. What an awful man Benjamin Sanders must be to write such filth. She couldn't wait to start it.

Downstairs, in the study, Paul had a fire going in the massive stone fireplace. The crackling cedar logs and the warmth and glow of the fire made this his favorite room.

Paul became totally absorbed in the book. It was interesting, factual and therefore exceedingly challenging to him as one of America's most popular preachers. It was up to him to defend the Holy Bible against the fierce attack of Professor Sanders.

The Trial of St. John

CHAPTER FOUR

THE DEFENDANT, THE PROSECUTOR and the court audience all stood respectfully when the Judge entered the courtroom.

"You may be seated." the bailiff called out.

The Judge smoothed his purple robe and sat down. He looked at the Prosecutor in his torn prison uniform and scrawny bare feet sticking out of his dirty sandals.

The Judge thought to himself: "What has the world come to? Almost 1600 years after the fall of Rome, there was Auschwitz. Had mankind learned nothing in all those years? They called the Romans barbarians for the death games at the Coliseum, but all those killed in the Coliseum would be just one day's toll in the gas chambers.

"Well Mr. Prosecutor, what horrors have you prepared for us this morning?"

"Your Honor, I do not enjoy this history lesson any more than you do, but it is essential for my case. The words of St. John echo through all the massacres the Jews have endured since the birth of Christianity. May I proceed?"

"Yes, yes. Let's get on with it." The judge settled back in his chair as the Prosecutor once more approached the witness box.

John was sitting stiffly in his chair, immaculately groomed as before. He was a handsome man, tall, distinguished with finely chiseled features.

"John, I am going to quote from your Gospel some of the things you said about Jews. I'd like you to confirm that you actually wrote those words." The Prosecutor picked up the King James version of the Bible and read from the Gospel of John.

John listened carefully. "Those are my words. Taken out of context as usual."

The Prosecutor smiled wearily. "Of course the quotes are out of context John. I do not believe the Judge would want me to recite your entire Gospel. You did accuse the Jews of being children of the Devil in Chapter Eight, verse 44 as I previously quoted and your description of the crucifixion clearly blames the Jews for his murder. According to your Gospel, the Jews were indeed a depraved, sinister people, a people who deserved to be punished."

John turned to the Judge. "Your honor, I have already explained the reason I wrote as I did. The Romans were in control of our world. They had just defeated the Jews after a long and very bloody war. The Jews were enemies of Rome. I sought to show that the Jews were our enemies also and therefore Rome could be our friend.

"It is a gross distortion to pick out one sentence from my Gospel. You need to judge my Gospel in its entirety, not by one sentence. My Gospel and the New Testament is about the wondrous work of Jesus Christ and the message of love he brought to the world. What if someone looked at the Constitution of the United States and claimed it was written to protect slavery. You could point to the clause that states African slaves were to be counted as 3/5ths of a person and the slave trade was to continue for 20 years. But that would not be the essence of the Constitution designed to protect freedom from tyranny.

"My Gospel must be judged in the period in which it was written. The period when Rome ruled the world. What happened to the Jews later were unintended consequences. I meant no harm. I wanted to save the Jews for a life eternal by converting them to worship Jesus."

The Prosecutor paced in front of the witness stand. "John, I understand your motive. Unfortunately, your words lived long after you. They became sacred, part of the Holy Bible."

John replied instantly: "I am honored that my work has been preserved. However, it was never my intention to have my words used to justify violence."

"I do believe you John, but in fact they were. Let me tell you about one man who was a devout Greek Orthodox Christian. His name was Bogdan Chmielnicki. In the year 1648, he led an army of Cossacks and peasants against the Polish nobles and against the Jews. The massacres of Jews went on for five years. Over 100,000 Jews were brutally murdered and 300 Jewish communities completely destroyed.

"Chmielnicki truly believed you John, that the Jews were children of the Devil. He not only killed them, he sadistically tortured them. I will spare you the details. They are all written down in Rabbi Berel Wein's authoritative book, *Triumph of Survival*.

"Chmielnicki has not been forgotten in the Ukraine. Berel Wein writes: 'A great heroic statue of Bogdan Chmielnicki stands in Kiev today as a monument to one of the leading butchers of mankind. As is often the case in human history, one man's butcher is another man's hero.' Rabbi Wein writes in a footnote: 'There is as of now (1990), still no monument in Kiev to the 35,000 Jews the Nazis murdered at Babi Yar. Statues are for the killers, not the victims.'"

John was obviously moved. He wiped his eyes. "That man was not a Christian. Our religion teaches love, not hate. You cannot blame me if Christians do not practice their religion and do not follow the teachings of Jesus Christ."

"But I do blame you John. For centuries Christians studied your Gospel and accepted your judgment that the Jews were an evil people. Unfortunately, your Gospel is still studied by Christians throughout the world. A new generation is being taught to hate Jews."

The Prosecutor walked to his table and picked up some notes. "John, I mentioned Babi Yar. Let me tell you about an eyewitness to that massacre. His name is Kurt Schmidt and he was a member of the Einsatzgruppe of the German Army. This was a special unit whose job was to find Jews and kill them. Kurt was 31 years old at the time of Babi Yar. As a young man, he had been a member of the Nazi Youth along with all of his friends. After high school, he worked in construction, got married, had a lovely little daughter. They lived in a comfortable apartment in Berlin and went to church every Sunday. Kurt loved his family and his dog. He liked to play soccer with his friends. Then on September 1, 1939 Germany invaded Poland and World War II began. Kurt was drafted and was a good soldier.

"On September 19, 1941 after a long battle, the German Army occupied Kiev, a key city in the Ukraine. Kurt's unit moved in to find the Jews who had not already fled the city. With the help of Ukrainian collaborators, they found them. From September 29th thru September 30th, the Einsatzgruppe rounded up 35,000 Jews. With submachine guns trained on them, the Jews were forced to march two miles to the deep ravine at Babi Yar. There they were forced to remove all their clothes and go down into the ravine. Kurt and his unit opened fire on the naked helpless Jews. Kurt aimed his gun at a mother holding her baby and killed them.

"John, you were there at Babi Yar. Kurt Schmidt was not shooting at human beings. He was killing Jews, those children of the Devil you wrote about. His priest and his parents told him that Jews were evil people. It was in the Bible so it had to be true. Adolf Hitler told him the Jews were subhuman and had to be eliminated before they infected the Master Race."

John rose from the witness chair and faced the Judge. "Your Honor, the Prosecutor is distorting the whole meaning of the New Testament. I was not at Babi Yar. What happened there was a hideous event perpetrated by evil men. Those men were not Christians. Christians believe in Jesus Christ who would abhor such sickening violence."

Once again the gavel came down with a loud bang.

"That will be all for today gentlemen. Court is adjourned until 10 AM sharp tomorrow."

The Judge quickly left the courtroom. He carried with him the vision of the Cossack massacre of the Jews and the horrors of Babi Yar.

Chapter

Sixteen

THE REVEREND PAUL HENRY Porter would have to be good today. Aside from the religious networks that carried his Sunday morning sermons, the premier program of CBS, *60 Minutes,* would take excerpts from his sermon for a special segment they would be doing on Christian activists.

The Thompsons had risked life in prison to stop a book critical of the Holy Bible. It was his duty to defend the Gospels, just as he went to war to defend the ideals of America.

Paul Henry stepped up to the podium. His wavy black hair was accented by the grey at the temples. His tall frame moved gracefully beneath the long black clerical robe. A hush fell over the audience. There was standing room only this Sunday morning.

The red light of the TV camera clicked on. Paul Henry began in his deep resonate voice: "The message of the New Testament is really very simple. Follow Jesus. Love one another. Have faith in our Lord Jesus Christ and you will be saved for life eternal.

"We have tried dear Jesus. We have tried. But how can we follow You when we are surrounded by sin? Schoolchildren selling dope, government officials stealing money, clergymen accused of rape, young girls having babies.

"The world is a mess dear Lord. Our streets are war zones, children being molested by those they trust, divorce is rampant. Millions of unborn babies have been killed. Hideous wars plague us throughout the world and the nuclear nightmare is still with us."

Reverend Paul Henry Porter was just warming up. He strode across the stage like a caged lion. His fury marked by the sweat on his brow. The TV cameras recorded every move.

"If you want to save your soul from eternal damnation, you must believe in our Lord Jesus."

"Amen." murmured the crowd.

"I didn't hear you," Paul Henry yelled back at them.

"Amen!" the audience shouted.

`"Do not whisper to the Lord. Shout His glory and sing His praise!"

"Amen! Amen!" The camera focused on a young woman whose face was radiant with joy. She was shouting "Amen!" at the top of her voice.

"Can the Lord hear you?" Paul Henry shouted back.

The fever was mounting. The crowd was ready. Paul Henry walked to the front of the stage.

"What did you say?"

"Amen! Amen!" The voices of all the good Christians rose to a crescendo of sound that shook the crystal chandeliers.

"Amen! Amen! Hallelujah!" Paul Henry shouted back to the crowd. He paced slowly across the stage.

"You cannot be saved by shouting Amen on Sunday mornings. You must truly believe in our Lord Jesus Christ. And how do you show your faith? How do you prove your love of Jesus? You must act as Christians. Show your love. Prove your faith. And resist the sinners.

"Do not sit idly by and let the sinners steal your faith, steal your country, corrupt your children. Satan does not sleep my friends. His evil hand is everywhere. There is blasphemy everywhere. Will you fight it?"

"Yes! Yes!" Some in the audience were on their feet. An elderly lady raised her fist, her face red with anger.

"Will you fight evil? Will you fight the Devil?"

More jumped to their feet

"Yes! Yes!"

Now the vast auditorium erupted with sound and movement. People were stomping their feet, clapping their hands, shouting to the Lord.

Paul Henry smiled broadly. Now they were his. He waited a few minutes for the clapping to subside and then continued: "There are teachers in our schools and professors in our universities who want to turn America into a godless society. We, who believe in the Bible, who believe in Jesus Christ, we are not stupid people. We know about Charles Darwin and his Theory of Evolution.

We do not oppose the teaching of evolution as long as it is taught as a theory, not as a fact. For the fact is that Darwin's theory of evolution has never been proven. *Origin of Species* was published in 1859. After more than a century of research, it still remains only a theory. It is only fair that students be told that there is another theory, that man was created by God and given an immortal soul.

"If we are but the next link in the evolution of the ape family, then man has no soul, no spiritual being. He is just an animal like the other animals in the zoo. Without God, there is no spiritual man, no absolute basis for moral conduct.

"In classrooms throughout our great nation, students of literature and history are taught that the Bible is just paper and ink. It is not. It is the word of God. If we mock the Bible, for what appear to be minor historical inconsistencies, we demean it. The Bible is spiritual and artistic Truth. It is the foundation of Christianity, the glue that holds our society together, the historical bedrock of America.

"If the Bible is considered just another old history book and God the invention of man, then we will be left with no absolute standard of morality. Without God, there is no moral law.

"What is right? What is wrong? Without Divine Law, without the God-given Ten Commandments, the only law is the law of the jungle: might makes right.

"Attack the Bible and you attack God. Attack God and you attack the moral code of civilized man. Destroy the Gospels and you destroy the Bible. Destroy the Bible and you destroy God's message to mankind. What is God's message? It is to love one another.

"Many politicians and teachers are trying to keep God from our children, to deny Jesus His rightful place in America. This is still a Christian country. Of course, give others the freedom to practice their own religions, but do not crucify the majority by the tyranny of the few. We too have rights. But we must fight for them. We must fight the lies they are telling our children about our Holy Bible. We want No More Lies! No More Lies!"

The audience caught the cue and began a fervent chant: "No More Lies! No More Lies!"

The camera shifted to the audience. The faces were young and old, black and white, men, women and children. All of them dedicated to Jesus, shouting their hearts out for the Reverend Paul Henry Porter.

Paul Henry raised his arms for quiet and resumed his sermon.

"We are against sin. We are against blasphemy. We are against the Devil. We know that. The world knows that. But that is not enough. It is not what we are against that will inspire men and women to follow Jesus. It is what we are for. And what are you for? What would you die for? We are for God. We are for our Holy Bible. We are for the Ten Commandments. We are for the family. We are for the United States of America!"

Applause, cheers, "Amen!" swept through the crowd. Paul Henry paused to wipe his brow. He walked to the front of the stage. No lectern could confine him. He had to feel the pulse of the people, to move close to them, to embrace them with all his fervor.

"We are living in an age of moral decay. Sex has become a sport instead of an act of love. Honesty in government, in business, in life is an endangered idea. Drugs corrupt our society breeding crime and dealing death. Hundreds of billions of dollars are spent on defense and yet we are helpless to stop the terror in some of our neighborhoods.

"For 60 years we have poured the wealth of our country into a war against poverty, but poverty still remains. The slums are worse, crime is worse, disease is worse and the schools are much worse. Millions of dollars are spent every year to murder the unborn. We cannot create life. What right do we have to destroy life?

"What has happened to us? Our generation is blessed with incredible knowledge and astounding technical skills. We can fly men to the moon, send pictures around the world in seconds. We are so smart and so troubled. There is a path to a better life on Earth. We know what it is. We must gather the courage to follow the laws of God. And what are the laws of God? They are here!"

Paul Henry raised the Bible over his head and waved it to the audience.

"Praise the Lord!" he shouted.

"Praise the Lord! Praise the Lord! Praise the Lord!" the crowd shouted with joyful enthusiasm.

Paul Henry paced across the stage soaking up the warm vibrations from the crowd. He was reaching them. Perhaps he was reaching the millions watching on television.

Perhaps he could make a difference, make America better, make his dream come true. He continued: "What can you do? Be active. Be concerned. Be vocal. There are teachers who are challenging our Bible. Confront them. Debate them. Do not let them conquer the minds of our children, our hope for the future.

"I'll give you an example, but there are hundreds more. Friends have told me about a professor at Lake Forest College in Illinois who tells his students that our Gospels are based on lies. Imagine, our Bible, the Bible that inspired the Pilgrims and our Founding Fathers is just a pack of lies. How disgraceful. How un–American.

"Now I have not met Professor Benjamin Sanders of Lake Forest College. I assume he is a good family man, but he is mistaken. He does not understand that you must study the Bible in its totality. You cannot pick out a sentence here and there and gloat over it. You must look at the total picture.

"Would you criticize *Hamlet* if Shakespeare erred on a few historical references? Of course not. *Hamlet* is a work of genius. Our Bible is the work of Almighty God who inspired the writers of our Gospels."

The crowd was jubilant. There was wild applause and a chorus of "Amen!" Paul Henry wiped his brow and looked squarely at the lens of the TV camera. "God bless you all and God bless America."

The church organist struck the chords on the new Allen organ and the Reverend Paul Henry Porter led his vast congregation in the singing of *"God Bless America"*. The youth choir behind him added their fervent voices.

The worshippers held hands and swayed together to the rhythm of the music

This was America. This is what he had fought for. Paul Henry left the podium. There were tears in his eyes.

Chapter

Seventeen

On Sunday mornings, Ben Sanders watched the Reverend Paul Henry Porter on the religious channel. He admired the reverend's style, his evangelical flair, his Biblical insights. Ben couldn't believe it when he heard his name singled out for attack. As soon as the program was over, Ben called his agent.

"Michael, did you happen to watch Channel 38 this morning?"

"No. I was watching the senator from Oregon sweat bullets on *Meet the Press*. They got him on video taking money from a Japanese lobbyist. Disgusting. You can't trust anyone these days."

"Well, I've got the Reverend Paul Henry Porter on tape. I tape his shows for my class on Christianity in America. He was really impressive today. He even gave me a plug."

"What do you mean?"

"He singled me out as an example of an evil influence on our children."

"Wow!" What is your Board of Trustees going to think about that?"

"I'm sure there will be some hollering and screaming, but I have tenure now. They're stuck with me."

"Unless they get you on a morals charge," Michael replied.

"I'm clean as a whistle. Rumor has it the girls in my class call me St. Benjamin."

"You must fight off all those beautiful coeds. How do you resist?"

"It's easy. I just remember that Michelle has a big butcher knife in the kitchen."

"Saint my foot," Michael laughed. "You're just a coward Ben and you better stay that way."

"I'm sure there will be some fireworks from the Reverend's sermon. Pity we can't publish *The Trial of St. John* so the public could understand the history behind my views."

"Damn pity," Michael agreed. "Until the FBI catches those kidnappers, it's just too dangerous."

"I know," Ben sighed. "So much for freedom of the press in America."

Chapter

Eighteen

"WHAT A STORY! AND we've got the scoop on it." Lori O'Connell was excited. It was her normal state. "Can you get the signs in the background?"

"Got them Lori. Ready when you are." Ed Carter was always ready. They were a good team. Lori with her perky smile and sweet personality used her wholesome good looks as a lethal weapon in Chicago's tough competition for TV viewers.

They were an odd couple. Lori, white, young, blonde — full of energy and outrage. Ed, black, calm, experienced — he'd seen it all before. Black and white in car number one for Channel 3 News in Chicago. Ready to roll, anytime, anywhere, any neighborhood.

"Okay Ed, let's do it." Lori saw the red button click on as Ed pointed the camera at her.

"This is Lori O'Connell reporting from the campus of Lake Forest College. As you can see in the background, hundreds of demonstrators have invaded this quiet, picturesque campus. From the signs on the dozens of buses parked nearby, the demonstrators come from churches throughout the Chicago area. Let's zero in and see the signs."

The crowd was chanting: "Shame on Ben. Let him go. Reverend Porter told us so."

As Lori and Ed moved closer to the crowd, Ed focused his camera on a tall, grey haired lady chanting with joyous dedication. She was carrying a placard neatly printed in large block letters: "Professor Sanders insults our Holy Bible."

The man next to her, marching with the zealous determination of a Crusader, waved his sign at the camera. It read: "Defend Jesus Christ." Lori signaled for the Crusader to come closer.

"Good morning sir. I'm Lori O'Connell from Channel 3 News. Could you tell us what is going on here?"

The man put his sign down like a knight sheathing his sword. "What's going on here is my Alma Mater has a professor defaming the Bible."

"What's his name?" Lori asked, handing the microphone to the Crusader.

"Benjamin Sanders, Professor of History. Can you imagine the gall of that man? He said the Gospels were based on lies!"

"Have you heard him say that?" Lori asked.

"Not personally. But yesterday on TV, Reverend Paul Henry Porter accused Professor Sanders of slandering the Bible."

"Did the Reverend say where he heard Professor Sanders say those things?"

The Crusader looked puzzled. "No. He said he never met Professor Sanders, but friends told him about what the Professor was teaching his students."

"Did the Reverend say who his friends were?" Lori persisted.

"Well no, he didn't say. But the Reverend wouldn't lie about such a terrible thing."

"I see," Lori said, smiling sweetly. "Thank you for talking to us."

The Crusader picked up his sign and marched defiantly back into the procession that was walking back and forth in front of Laird Hall where Professor Sanders had his office.

Lori resumed her live report for Channel 3 News. "We will try to get a statement from Professor Sanders as soon as possible. This is Lori O'Connell returning you to our studio in Willis Tower." The red light clicked off.

"How was it Ed?"

"You were great Lori. You asked that Crusader fellow some good questions."

Lori and Ed walked through the line of chanting demonstrators, past the security guards and up the stairs to the office of Professor Sanders.

"Keep the camera rolling Ed. We might get some interesting footage."

At the reception desk, Lillian retained her composure. This was the most excitement Lake Forest College had seen since Madonna gave a concert here.

"May I help you?" Lillian asked the pretty blonde girl and the big black man lugging the camera.

"We would like to see Professor Sanders," Lori said in her most assertive voice.

"Is he expecting you?" Lillian asked, trying to protect her boss from these intruders.

"He might be with all the commotion outside."

"And who shall I say would like to see him without an appointment?"

Lori felt insulted that the silver-haired receptionist didn't know her name.

"Lori O'Connell from Channel 3 News."

Of course, Lillian knew who she was. The pretty face from Channel 3 News, but Lillian wanted to bring Lori down a peg or two. Lillian picked up the phone.

"Professor Sanders, there is a reporter here, Lori O'Connell from Channel 3 News and a cameraman. Do you have time to see them today?"

"It's Okay, Lillian. Send them in. We might as well get this over with."

Lori and Ed walked into Ben's office. Ed kept the camera rolling. Ben got up from his desk and walked over to shake hands with Lori and Ed.

"You're the first reporters here today," Ben said with a smile. "I guess more will be coming."

"You can count on that Professor Sanders. This is big news for our viewers," Lori said as she took the chair in front of Ben's desk. Ed positioned the camera so it took in both Professor Sanders and Lori.

"May I ask you some questions about the demonstrations outside?" Lori began.

"Certainly," Ben replied.

"Did you really slander the Bible like one of the demonstrators told us?"

"I never slandered the Bible."

"The TV evangelist, Reverend Paul Henry Porter, said you did."

"He's mistaken."

Lori needed some longer answers. She tried a different approach.

"Professor, could you explain to our audience what your views are on the New Testament?"

Ben smiled at the pretty blonde reporter. "That is usually the subject of my two hour lecture, but I'll be happy to highlight the main points. I believe the New Testament is one of the most important books in the history of Western Civilization. I believe that Jesus of Nazareth, the Jewish Rabbi from Galilee, to be one of the most remarkable and influential figures in world history. His love and compassion for his fellow man should be the ideal for all of us to follow.

"Unfortunately, there are contradictions in the Gospels. While Jesus preached love, the Gospel of John is full of hate for the Jews."

"Are you blaming the Bible for the Holocaust?" Lori asked, hoping to get a sensational story.

"That is a debatable idea," Ben replied. "Hitler and the German people must carry that terrible shame. But the groundwork was prepared by centuries of anti-Semitism, anti-Semitism that is rampant in the New Testament. It is as if you poured gasoline on the floor of a building. If no one lit a match, there would be no fire. Hitler lit the match. Anti-Semitism was there, waiting to explode."

"Thank you for your views professor", Lori said, getting up to say goodbye. The camera light clicked off. Lori extended her hand. "Thank you, professor."

"You are most welcome Lori. Come see me anytime." Ed and Ben also shook hands and said their goodbyes. As Lori was about to leave the office, Ben said:

"Lori, may I ask you a question?"

"Sure."

"When you went to Sunday school and church, what did you learn about the Jews?"

"The Jews killed Jesus Christ," Lori answered honestly.

"Did you learn to hate Jews?"

"Of course. Everyone did."

"Do you still hate Jews?"

"Certainly not!"

"Why not?" Ben persisted.

"I work with Jews every day. They are great. Almost as much fun as the Irish." Lori's blue eyes sparkled and she gave Ben a mischievous smile. "I think you are right professor. The Jews got a bum rap. Keep up the good work. Maybe the Pope will get the message."

"He already has, Lori. It's not the Pope that's the problem. It's all the millions of Christians who still believe every word in the Bible is the Gospel truth."

"Why don't you write a book professor so we can study your views," Ed asked seriously.

"I have Ed."

"Where can I get a copy?"

"I'm afraid we are having a problem getting it published," Ben said sadly.

"Well, good luck professor," Ed said as the Channel 3 News team headed back to Chicago.

Chapter

Nineteen

MAX LEVI PUT THE manuscript down. He looked out his picture window to the restless lake. Mrs. Sanders had sent him *The Trial of St. John* several weeks ago. This Sunday morning he finally had a chance to read it as he had promised. He had planned to only skim through pages to be polite, but it was an intriguing book. The Jews were indeed the Chosen People, chosen to suffer.

The details of Auschwitz were horrifying, but Max Levi did not need to read about them. He was there. No words on paper could ever capture the sheer terror and hell he saw with his own eyes. Now he was ready to finish the book.

The Trial of St. John

CHAPTER FIVE

THE JUDGE WAS GROWING weary of this long trial. His hopes for mankind had been shattered. During his lifetime of empire-building, he had thought that each succeeding generation would build on the accomplishments of the past. That the life of his children and their children far into the future would be better because he had worked so hard and so bravely to build a strong Rome.

But alas, he discovered that Rome had crumbled and man had crumbled with it. History was a tiresome record of man's failures. He banged down the gavel on what he hoped would be the final day of this gruesome trial.

"Are you ready, Mr. Prosecutor?"

"Yes, your Honor."

"Well then, let's get on with it."

The Prosecutor walked to the witness box to once again confront John. "Today John, I want to discuss with you the so-called friends of the Jews. What did America do to help the Jews of Europe as they were being hunted by the Nazis?"

John replied cautiously, "I've read that the Americans were a very religious people. Surely, they should have followed the words of Jesus: 'Love thy neighbor as thy self.'"

"If only they had John, if only they had. Let me tell you about one specific case. November 9, 1938 was Kristallnacht, the Night of Broken Glass. That night Hitler's thugs set fire to every synagogue in Germany. Thousands of Jewish homes and businesses were looted. Jewish shop windows were shattered, hundreds of Jews murdered and 30,000 Jewish men arrested and sent to Dachau. After that night, there was no doubt the Jews needed to escape from Germany.

"Adolf Hitler gave the Jews permission to leave Germany as long as they turned over their wealth to the German Government. But where could they go? No nation wanted them.

"Three months after Kristallnacht, in January, 1939, a German-born Catholic, Senator Robert F. Wagner of New York, introduced the Child Refugee Bill on the floor of the United States Senate. The bill would allow 10,000 Jewish children to be admitted to the USA in 1939 and 10,000 to be admitted in 1940. All the children would be under the age of 14 and would be adopted temporarily by American families. All the costs would be borne by Jewish organizations and the children would not be permitted to work to avoid any charge of unfair labor.

"In testimony before a Congressional committee considering the bill, famed newscaster Quentin Reynolds, just back from Germany, predicted all the Jews in Germany would be killed by Hitler and thus the Child Refugee Bill was a matter of life or death.

"Opposition to the bill came from 115 patriotic societies organized as the American Coalition. The Coalition included the American Legion, Veterans of Foreign Wars and the American Christian Crusade. Opponents of the bill cited the results of a *Fortune* magazine poll of April, 1939. The question posed was: 'If you were a member of Congress would you vote yes or no on the Child Refugee Bill?'"

"The results were overwhelming: 83% said no. 8.3% said 'don't know' and only 8.7% said yes. The Child Refugee Bill did not pass. 20,000 Jewish children who could have been saved from Hitler's "Final Solution" were denied permission to come to the United States of America. Why would Americans want children of the Devil to come to their country?"

"That is unbelievable," John said sincerely. "What a horrible tragedy that those children were not saved."

"But don't you see John, your words guided their actions. Those fine American Christians had studied the Bible. They believed what you wrote about the Jews. The Jews killed Christ and the Jews were children of the Devil. How could you expect them to let those terrible Jews into America?

"The very anti-Semitic U.S. State Department ordered our embassies in Europe not to issue visas to Jews. Arthur D. Morse, a former CBS executive, detailed the State Department's war against the Jews in his well-documented book, *While Six Million Died, A Chronicle of American Apathy.*

"Several non-Jewish officials in the U.S. Treasury Department led by Josiah DuBois wrote one of the most amazing documents on file with the U.S. government. Their 18-page report was titled: *Report to the Secretary on the Acquiescence of this Government in the Murder of the Jews.* As a result of this report, President Franklin Roosevelt finally established the War Refugee Board in 1944. It was too little and too late to save thousands of Jews who could have been saved."

John leaned forward in his chair and pointed his finger at the Prosecutor. "It's not my fault that America would not save the Jews. If they were good Christians they would have followed the words of Jesus and showed compassion for the refugees."

"I wish they had, I truly wish they had," the Prosecutor replied.

"Let me give you one more story about the compassion of the Americans. On May 13, 1939, the German ocean liner, the *St. Louis,* set sail from Hamburg, Germany to Havana, Cuba. There were 937 passengers on board, most of them German Jews fleeing Hitler. When the ship reached Havana, the Cuban government refused to allow the ship to dock even though the passengers had proper visas. The German ship captain set sail for Miami.

"The *St. Louis* dropped anchor outside Miami harbor. The passengers lined the railing and marveled at the gleaming skyline of Miami, their hope for freedom, their hope for life. The captain waited for permission to dock. The days went by. In Washington, D.C., Jewish leaders begged President Roosevelt to grant that permission. Eleanor Roosevelt also pleaded with her husband to allow the 937 passengers to escape from Hitler.

"On the other side, southern Senators, important for FDR's legislative agenda, told the President not to let the Jews into America. If he did, he would lose votes in the Senate. Public opinion as reflected in the Fortune magazine poll was overwhelming opposed to letting those children of the Devil, those terrible Jews into the country. Permission to dock in Miami was denied. The *St. Louis* sailed back to Europe on June 6, 1939. Most of the passengers were eventually killed in the Holocaust."

The Prosecutor approached the witness. "I want to thank you John for your attention and your honest answers. You seem to be a fine gentleman. Too bad you wrote those words about the Jews."

The Prosecutor turned to the Judge. "I'm finished with this witness your honor." The Prosecutor walked slowly back to his table and slid quietly into his chair. He had done his job. He had shown the Judge that the Gospel of John had sown the seeds of anti-Semitism that led to the persecution of the Jews throughout the ages and eventually to the Holocaust. The only just verdict would be that the Gospel of John was guilty as charged.

"Thank you, Mr. Prosecutor," the Judge said. "I'll review all the testimonies and present my decision in a few days. Before we adjourn, I will ask John to say a few, very few final words. John, if you would please give us your view of this trial."

John stood and faced the audience. It was a strange audience. Some wore the garments he knew as a lad. Others wore clothing from the period of the Crusades, from the Spanish Inquisition, from the villages of 17th century Poland. There were lavish costumes from the Paris of Louis XIV and coarse, heavy garments from the land of the Czars. Americans were in the audience with modern fashions and Israelis were there also, informal and proud.

"Your Honor," John said in a firm resonate voice. "We have heard a litany of horrors these past few days. I weep for the victims of cruelty and murder. Obviously, mankind has not learned the lesson that Jesus brought to all of us: to love one another. Now the Prosecutor has sought to link one sentence from my Gospel to all the murders of Jews throughout the ages. Frankly, that is absurd. The Prosecutor's attempt to cast the blame on the Bible for all the terrible persecutions of the Jews is very dangerous. His remarks demean the Bible. My Gospel is part of the New Testament. You cast doubt on my Gospel because of one sentence out of thousands of words and you cast doubt on the validity of the Bible about the true story of Jesus Christ and the hope and love he brought into this world.

"I am not guilty of the massacres of the Jews. The Bible is not guilty. The ones who are guilty are the ones who committed the murders. If you are told to shoot a Jew and you do, who is guilty? The man who pulls the trigger or the man who told him to do so. In any court of law, the man who pulls the trigger is the guilty one. It is a question of personal responsibility. You are responsible for your actions.

"When Adolph Eichmann was put on trial in Jerusalem for his role in the murder of millions of Jews, what was his defense? He was just following orders, he was not responsible. The jury did not accept that defense and Eichmann was hanged.

"You want to know who to blame for the massacre of the Jews during the Crusades? Blame the Crusaders, not the Bible. For the tortures and burning alive at the stake during the Grand Inquisition, blame Torquemada, not the Bible. For the brutal murder of the Jews by the Cossacks, blame the Cossacks, not the Bible. For America's refusal to accept Jewish refugees, blame the Americans, not the Bible. For the horrors of the Holocaust, blame Adolf Hitler and the Nazis, not the Bible.

"Before there was a New Testament people had no trouble finding excuses to slaughter one another. Jews were not the only ones killed senselessly and brutally. Catholics and Protestants murdered each other since the days of Martin Luther and continued to do so during the 20th Century in Northern Ireland. All the nations of Europe found reasons to hate their neighbors and wage devastating wars. Jews were not the only ones burned at the stake. Think of that gallant heroine, Joan of Arc, and her cruel death. Think of the Great Witch Hunt in Europe during the 16th and 17th centuries when 70,000 so-called witches, mostly women, were burned alive at the stake.

"Frankly, I never thought my words would bring any harm to the Jews. I knew how the Romans had utterly crushed the Jews, had executed their leaders, sold thousands into slavery and demolished their magnificent Temple. I thought the Jews would just vanish into history like the Samaritans or the Phoenicians. If I were to write my Gospel today, I would omit all reference to the Jews. But I cannot change history. I cannot rewrite the Bible. Either the Bible stands as written or it is totally destroyed.

"Suppose you were on a crowded lifeboat and someone points out a worm infested plank on the bottom of the boat. It is a disgusting sight and some ask you to remove that plank. If you remove that plank, the boat will sink. Perhaps there are parts of the Bible we wish were not there. But, if we remove those parts, the Bible is destroyed. The Holy Bible is a unity. You cannot pick what chapters you like and which ones you dislike. It is all or nothing.

"Should it be nothing, would the world be better off? Would the world be a better place if there was no story of Jesus Christ? Would the world be better if we did not know that once upon a time there walked among us an extraordinary man who had a noble vision of peace and brotherhood?

"I urge your honor to keep in mind the inspiration, the lofty ideals and the hope instilled by the Holy Bible. I am proud to be a part of it. There can be only one just verdict in this case. I am not guilty, the Bible is not guilty. Only those who committed the sinful and terrible tortures and murders are guilty. Their actions were directly contrary to the teachings of Jesus Christ.

"Thank you, Your Honor."

Max Levi closed the manuscript. He would have to read the last chapter tomorrow. It was midnight and a sudden weariness settled over him like a dark cloud. Why hadn't this book been published? It was good, very good. Perhaps with a little help from Max Levi *The Trial of St. John* could be brought to life.

Chapter

Twenty

"HISTORY DEPARTMENT," LILLIAN ANSWERED in her usual crisp voice.

"Hi Lillian, it's Michelle. Is Ben in?"

"Yes he is Mrs. Sanders. I'll ring the professor for you."

Ben picked up immediately. "Hi Honey, what's up?"

"You said to call if I had a new brainstorm. Well, I have one."

"You certainly are a persistent lady, aren't you? Okay dear, what's your new idea?"

"Like manna from heaven, you got a letter from Max Levi."

"Max Levi from the synagogue?" Ben asked with surprise.

"Yes! Max Levi, the speaker at our Yom Ha Shoah service. Max Levi, survivor of Auschwitz, Max Levi, multi-multimillionaire. That Max Levi."

"Okay. I've got the picture. What did he write me about?"

"Remember after the service, I asked if I could send him your manuscript? Well, I did send it, over a month ago. I never heard from him until today."

"Okay, Okay. What did he write?" Ben asked impatiently.

"Listen to this: 'I read your manuscript and I believe your book is important, very important. It is too late to help the victims of Auschwitz, but it is not too late to help their descendants. Please call me if you would like my assistance in getting your book published. Cordially, Max Levi.'"

"Bravo for Max! That's a wonderful letter, but I don't see how he can help us. He's in the retail business. He knows designer sportswear. What does he know about blackmail?"

"A lot more than we do Ben. He's rich and famous and powerful. I think we should call him."

"Why don't you take care of it Michelle? I don't want to be disappointed again."

"Just leave it to me. I'm pretty comfortable around millionaires after that great sale to Howard Edward Greenfield."

"That was a beauty Michelle. I think he has his eye on you."

"Now why would you say that?"

"Remember the gorgeous plant he sent you? I thought you were supposed to give the buyer a gift, not the other way around."

"Well, Howard was very special. Kinda cute too, don't you think?" Michelle teased.

"He's alright if you go for guys that get their kicks from pork bellies."

"Actually, I prefer sexy authors. I'm in the mood for one right now. Why don't you come home early?"

"Well, if I can break away from the pretty coeds waiting for me, I'll try to make it a short day."

"Tell your pretty coeds 'hands off' or I'll strangle them with their miniskirts."

"You are possessive today my sweet."

"Not today Ben, every day!"

"Sounds exciting," Ben laughed.

"It will be, I promise. Hate to say goodbye, but I've got a millionaire to call."

"Okay Honey. Good luck."

Ben smiled as he hung up the phone. He was so lucky he had Michelle. So glad that he hid those handcuffs. But why was he still keeping them? Just to prove that he could resist the seductive Cindy Cunningham. At least, he could resist her for now.

Michelle called Max Levi's private phone number he had included with his letter.

"Mr. Levi's residence." It was a deep male voice with a heavy European accent.

Probably the butler, Michelle guessed. "This is Mrs. Benjamin Sanders. Mr. Levi wrote to call his number regarding my husband's book."

"Oh yes. *The Trial of St. John.* Excellent book. Mr. Levi allowed me to read it. Impressive research."

"Thank you, Mr......?"

"Mr. Vogel. I'm Mr. Levi's home secretary. Mr. Levi is at his downtown office. If you leave me your phone number, I'll have Mr. Levi call you."

"Thank you, Mr. Vogel." Michelle left her number.

An hour later, the phone rang.

"Mrs. Sanders, this is Max Levi. I see you received my letter."

"Yes we did Mr. Levi. Thank you very much. It was so kind of you to offer your help."

"How can I be of help Mrs. Sanders?"

"I'm afraid it's a long story. Would it be possible to meet with you?"

"How's tonight at 8? You know my address."

"Your home is a landmark in Highland Park, Mr. Levi. 8 o'clock will be fine. Thank you so much."

"Good. I'll see you then." The phone clicked off. Max Levi did not waste time with chit chat.

The Levi home was situated on five acres of wooded land, high on a bluff overlooking Lake Michigan. The house could not even be seen from the street. The driveway was blocked by a high wrought iron gate. Mounted atop the gate was a television camera so the visitors could be seen as well as heard as they buzzed for admittance.

Michelle announced herself into the speaker box and the electronically controlled gate immediately swung open. She drove down a long lane lined with giant oaks and graceful willow trees. A wide circular driveway led her to a large gothic brick and stone mansion.

Mr. Vogel was waiting for her by the oversized double doors. "So nice to meet you Mrs. Sanders. I'm Adam Vogel. Mr. Levi is waiting for you in the library. Please follow me."

Adam Vogel was 60, stocky build, almost bald, wore steel-rimmed glasses and had a gracious Old World charm about him. Michelle liked him.

"This is magnificent!" Michelle exclaimed as she entered the library. In all her years showing homes on the North Shore, she had never seen a room like this. The library was huge, two stories tall and completely filled with books. Books lined three of the walls from floor to ceiling. A balcony on the second story level made access to every book possible with the help of ladders on wheels that were attached to guide rails. The fourth side of the room was all glass overlooking Lake Michigan. Floodlights illuminated the waves as they crashed against the seawall.

"Welcome to my favorite room Michelle."

"Thank you, Mr. Levi."

"Please, just call me Max. Now would you like a drink or some coffee?"

"No, thank you."

Adam Vogel closed the library door as he left Michelle and Max standing by the window watching the waves in their tireless quest to consume the shore.

"Please, Michelle, if you sit here," Max said motioning to an antique upholstered side chair, "we can watch the lake try to destroy my property."

"What a horrible thought," Michelle said.

"Don't worry. I can handle it," Max smiled. "I just put a sign on the beach, "No Trespassing" and the waves go away. Every time."

Max sat in the companion side chair and turned it so he was facing Michelle. "Now, please tell me why *The Trial of St. John* has not been published."

Michelle related the entire story of the kidnapping of Jenny and threat to kill her if Ben's book was ever published.

"Obviously, we need to catch the kidnappers and remove the threat from your family," Max replied as he pondered the problem.

"Don't tell me you're a detective also," Michelle asked in amazement. "The FBI hasn't found a clue yet."

"Well, the FBI has many cases to handle. Certainly your case is still open, but it is not the top priority. No one was hurt. Jenny is back."

"I can assure you it is a top priority in our home. We feel we are being watched all the time. And we worry about Jenny every day."

All of a sudden, Michelle began to weep. She was so embarrassed, but she just could not stop.

Max came to her with a large handkerchief and put his arm around her shoulder.

"Please excuse me. I didn't mean to burden you with our problem," Michelle managed to say between sobs.

"It's Okay my dear. Remember, I asked if I could help and I believe I can."

"But how can you if the police and the FBI haven't been able to find the kidnappers?"

"It's a matter of motivation and money. I've had some experience in matters like this."

"You have?" Michelle said, drying her tears.

"Yes. I helped finance the search for Adolf Eichmann. The whole world was looking for him, but we found him. The Israeli Mossad found him."

"Can you really help us?" Michelle said hopefully. "There don't seem to be any clues at all."

"There are always clues. You just have to dig deep for them. You met Adam Vogel, my assistant. He was a top investigator for the Mossad. He'll be in touch with you."

Michelle got up to say goodbye and shake hands with Max Levi, millionaire "*mensch*." Instead, she hugged him as if he were her father and would fix all her hurts.

On the drive home, Michelle felt relieved. Somehow she felt that Max Levi and Adam Vogel could do it. They could find the fanatics that had so frightened the Sanders family. She didn't know how they could find kidnappers who left no trail, but Adolf Eichmann had not left a trail either.

Michelle couldn't wait to tell Ben the good news. They had a new friend, a powerful friend, a millionaire friend.

"God bless you Max Levi. God bless you."

Chapter

Twenty-One

ADAM VOGEL CALLED MICHELLE the next day. He asked her to arrange for Jenny and her friend, Rachel Jacobs, to be at the Sanders' home that afternoon at 4 p.m. He would like to interview them together. At precisely 4 p.m. Adam Vogel arrived. Michelle introduced him to the girls and they all settled in the den.

Jenny told her story and Rachel added the brief part of what she had seen. Adam had placed his Sony recorder on the coffee table so he could review their stories. Michelle gave Adam the sketches the police artist had made of the delivery lady. Adam took from his briefcase two pads of drawing paper and two boxes of colored pencils. The girls look at him with surprise.

"What's that for?" Jenny asked.

"I want you girls to give me the most important clue in this case," Adam said with a smile.

"What's that?" Michelle asked totally bewildered by what clue the police had missed.

"The flowers, Mrs. Sanders. We're going to trace the flowers. I'll canvas all the florist shops until we find the one that sold the flowers that the delivery lady was holding. They may have some information about the customer who bought them."

"Girls," Adam turned to Jenny and Rachel, I need you to draw a picture of the flowers the lady was carrying."

"I'm a terrible artist," Rachel complained.

"Do the best you can. Your drawings are not for the Art Institute. They might help the sales clerk remember that customer."

"What a wonderful idea Adam," Michelle said delighted that someone was actively working the case.

Four days later, Adam and Max Levi were in the library. It was dusk outside. The waves were gently licking the shore. Adam handed Max an 8 x 10 glossy photo.

"That's the girl."

"Adam, you haven't lost your touch. How did you do it?"

"The usual way: shoe leather and luck. It wasn't hard to find the florist with the pictures the girls drew. At least the kidnappers had style. They bought a very expensive arrangement of orchids and tiger lilies. A saleslady at Tina's Floral and Gift Shop identified the flowers and the police sketch of the lady Jenny had talked to."

"That was the shoe leather part. Where did the luck come in?" Max asked as he studied the photo.

"The luck was that Tina's is a pretty thriving business. Not just flowers, but expensive gifts and crystal. Last year, they had a burglary. Lost some very valuable pieces and a few thousand dollars."

"That's the luck?" Max asked, knowing there was more to come.

"The luck was that Tina had security cameras installed. She gave the security company permission to show me the film for the day that Jenny was kidnapped. There were several good shots of the mystery lady. I had a photo lab enlarge those shots and made up a few dozen copies. I left copies around town with some of the shady folks I know.

"You still keep up your contacts don't you Adam," Max said approvingly.

Adam continued, pleased at his success. "The lady's name is Dawn Reynolds. The madam who books her runs the most expensive escort business in town. Her girls get $500 an hour and only go out with top politicians, entertainers, sports figures and business executives.

"With a little Old World charm and quite a few of your fine American dollars, I discovered Dawn is in France now."

"Wonderful Adam. Great work! Give yourself a bonus."

"I know where she is in France," Adam said, "but I'm not sure how we can get her back. I would hate to kidnap a beautiful kidnapper."

"I don't think we will have to do that," Max said as he picked up his smartphone. "I bet the right man could lure her back here and I know just the man for the job."

Chapter
Twenty-Two

LIFE IN THE FAST lane is a bore, Dawn thought to herself. She was stretched out on her lounge chair on the beach at the plush Hotel Pierre in Cannes. Her chair, towels and drinks were under the benevolent supervision of Andre, the beach attendant who treated her like a movie star. It was a natural mistake. She was gorgeous, obviously very rich from the overly generous tips she gave everyone and was definitely American. She was also alone.

Andre was tall, dark and handsome. Perhaps 18 or 19 years old. After a week at the hotel, Andre had offered himself to her. Dawn smiled at the recollection.

"Mademoiselle must be lonely in France," Andre had said as he brought her an afternoon screwdriver, heavy on the orange juice, light on the vodka.

"Yes, Andre. It is lonely, but sometimes a person just has to get away. I like it here."

"Perhaps mademoiselle would like it even better if she had a man friend?"

"Perhaps," Dawn admitted.

Andre straightened up. "Mademoiselle, if I may be so bold I would be honored to be your escort."

"Andre, come here." He had knelt beside her lounge chair. Dawn leaned over and kissed him on both checks. "That was the sweetest offer I've had all week. Thank you Andre, but I think you should save yourself for your girlfriend."

"But Mademoiselle," Andre protested, "there is enough of me for both of you."

Dawn had laughed heartily, sat up and gave Andre a smack on his behind.

"Get back to work Andre and thanks anyway," Dawn had said.

That was days ago and the most fun Dawn had had in France. Pretty sad, she thought. The only proposition she had received on the romantic Riviera was from a teenager.

As Dawn lay daydreaming, a shadow fell over her face. She looked up and saw a sexy guy with wavy black hair and grey eyes.

"Pardon me miss, the beach attendant asked me to drop this towel off to you on my way to the water."

"He is a sly one, isn't he?" Dawn laughed.

The man sat down on the sand beside her.

"The French are so romantic," he said. "They can't bear the sight of a beautiful woman sitting alone on the beach. Would you mind some company?"

"Not at all. Andre has standing orders to send all available men this way."

"You must be very busy then,"

"Not really. Andre is very protective. He screens the prospects thoroughly. In fact, you're the first to pass inspection. How did you do it?"

"Cost me ten dollars to find out your name was Dawn Reynolds."

"I would have told you for free."

"Story of my life. I just throw money away."

"You must have a lot of it to squander on such generous tips," Dawn teased.

As she studied the man next to her, Dawn wondered if it had been a mistake to keep her name. She had thought of changing it, but it would be quite a hassle to get new identity papers, forged passport and all. Besides, she was sure no one would be looking for her in France.

Wilbur Thompson had kept his promise. Jenny had not been hurt and was home safe and sound. No one had a clue who the kidnappers were. Dawn would stay in Europe for about a year until all the fuss about that Bible book just faded away.

"My name is Howard Edward Greenfield. I'm a rich, eligible American bachelor looking for a beautiful woman to dine with me tonight."

"You're probably an unemployed beach bum looking for a rich widow to swindle her out of her fortune," Dawn teased.

"Ah, you've read about me then," Howard laughed.

Great laugh, Dawn thought. The chemistry was good.

"How about a swim?" Howard asked eagerly.

"No thanks. I'm considering a proposal to dine with a rich American tonight and I don't want to muss my hair."

"I'm sure he wouldn't mind."

"You go ahead, but do come back."

"Then you will join me tonight?"

"I'm thinking about it."

Howard ran off to the cold, blue Mediterranean.

"Thank you God," Dawn said softly. This guy is gorgeous and fun. Of course she would go out with him tonight, every night, all night. Dawn watched Howard's arms rise and fall as he stroked slowly and rhythmically through the water. She squeezed some Coppertone into the palm of her hand a rubbed it gently on her thighs and legs. It felt sensuous to caress her body. It would feel even better when Howard did it.

Dawn stood up and studied the competition. The beach was fairly crowded. The French Riviera was a summer mecca for American and European tourists. The American girls were easy to spot. They wore the tops of their bikinis. The Europeans did not. The young French, Italian and German girls ran through the sand with their breasts bobbing tantalizing in front of attentive male spectators.

Dawn wondered about the cultural differences. Wearing their bikini tops seem to indicate that American girls were uptight about sex, uncomfortable with their sexual longings. Probably a carryover from their Puritan ancestors. It would be a good conversation topic with Howard. Might as well discuss human sexuality before jumping into bed with him. The idea of Howard making love to her sent tingles down her spine. She wanted him desperately.

Howard came back, water dripping from his taunt body like glistening bubbles.

"Welcome back," Dawn smiled.

"It's cold out there," Howard shivered as he caught the towel Dawn tossed him.

"Well, have you decided to gamble on dinner with me tonight?"

"I'd be delighted Mr. Greenfield."

"7 o'clock Okay?"

"Fine with me, but a little early for the French?"

"We're not dining with the French," Howard replied.

"We're not? I see. You're going to fly me to London on your private jet."

"You're close. We'll join some American friends on their yacht and cruise to Monte Carlo."

"On their yacht? Your friends? Monte Carlo?"

"I do have friends, you know," Howard replied with his special laugh.

"You gotta be kidding. You mean Andre really sent me a winner? Seriously, what should I wear tonight?"

"Seriously, your evening yacht dress would be just fine."

Howard extended his hand and pulled Dawn up from her chair.

"See the ship with the American flag?"

Dawn peered eagerly over Howard's outstretched arm pointing into the crowded harbor. The rich of the world seemed to congregate at Cannes. One yacht was more magnificent than the next.

"I'm afraid I can't make out the flags," Dawn said sadly.

"Trust me it's a beaut. You'll love it. I'll pick you up at seven at your hotel."

"Fine. I'll be ready. And Howard…"

"Yes?"

"Thank you!"

As Howard left the beach, Dawn blew a kiss to him.

Howard appeared promptly at 7 p.m. Dawn was waiting for him in the lobby. She was a vision of loveliness. She had on a short black sleeveless cocktail dress that displayed her shapely legs and accented her bare shoulders. She wore a single strand of pure white pearls. Dawn swirled slowly for Howard's approval.

"Wow! The back's as sexy as the front," he whispered. The back of her Valentino original was open down to her waist. The dress was designed to be worn braless and Dawn's smooth tanned skin seemed to invite further exploration.

Howard had told the truth. The taxi drove them to Pier 6 where they transferred to a motor launch to take them to the yacht.

"There she is." Howard pointed to a sleek ship with an American flag flapping in the evening breeze. It was the *Cocoa Bean*.

"What a weird name for a ship," Dawn said in surprise.

"Not strange at all," Howard replied. "The owner is Sheldon Waxman, <u>The</u> Sheldon Waxman."

"Should I know him?" Dawn searched her memory, but Sheldon Waxman drew a blank.

He's a legend in Chicago. Three years ago he made 21 million dollars trading cocoa futures. One million of that he made in one day! And then he quit. He lost his nerve. He reasoned that if he could make so much money so fast, he might lose it just as fast. Of course, he was right. We can lose just as big and fast as we can win."

"We?" Dawn said as the launch pulled alongside the *Cocoa Bean*.

"That's my business. I'm a trader in Chicago. That's where I met Sheldon."

"What do you trade?" Dawn asked as the sailors secured the lines and lowered the steps to the launch.

"What do I trade?" Howard repeated. "I trade everything, but basically, I buy and sell the future."

"I see," Dawn said in a puzzled voice. This was not the time for a lesson in international economics. She'd save that for another night. Tonight she was only interested in one future, her own. And her future was looking very bright as she ascended the steps to the *Cocoa Bean*.

It was a small party of friendly people, mostly Americans, with their wives or girlfriends.

"And this is Sheldon Waxman," Howard said completing the circle of introductions.

"Sheldon, say hello to my new friend Dawn Reynolds."

"Delighted you could join us Dawn."

Sheldon reminded Dawn of the Pillsbury doughboy on the old TV commercials. He was short, wore glasses and had wild red hair.

"What brings you to the Rivera?" Sheldon asked as he motioned to a uniformed attendant.

"Before you answer," Sheldon continued, "why don't you tell Franklin what you'd like to drink?"

"I'd like a Fuzzy Navel."

"A Fuzzy Navel?" Sheldon laughed. "Sounds kinky."

"Not really," Dawn smiled. "It's just peach schnapps with orange juice and a little vodka.

The drink is Okay. I order it because I like the name."

"Right away, Miss Reynolds," Franklin left for the bar and a Fuzzy Navel.

"How did he know my name?" Dawn asked in surprise.

"For every party, Franklin has a copy of the guest list," Sheldon explained. Next to each name, he notes their favorite drink. If you come back another time, Franklin will bring you a Fuzzy Navel as soon as you are on deck."

"How efficient," Dawn said, relieved that it was not unusual for a crew member to know her name. When you have been involved in a kidnapping, you get a little paranoid.

"So Dawn," Sheldon resumed his quiz, "what brings you to sunny France?"

"The usual reason for a single woman. I thought I might meet a rich bachelor on the beach."

"Well, Howard will have to do until you find one," Sheldon laughed. "You see, Howard is rich today, but he can be broke tomorrow if he doesn't get out of the crazy commodity business. You two have fun while I check on the other guests. Howard, why don't you show Dawn around the *Cocoa Bean*?"

"Your Fuzzy Navel, Miss Reynolds," Franklin said without a smile.

"Thank you, Franklin." When he left, Dawn and Howard strolled the deck.

"I see you're on Franklin's permanent drink list," Howard said.

"I suppose if I decide to change drinks, I'll screw up the whole system," Dawn said as she was admiring the beautiful ship.

"I'm sure Franklin can handle it," Howard replied.

"He doesn't look like a Franklin," Dawn mused.

"What do you mean?"

"A Franklin should be tall and elegant. Aristocratic, like Franklin Roosevelt. This Franklin is heavy, dark, mysterious. He looks more like a wrestler than a waiter."

"You're very perceptive Dawn. Franklin is much more than a waiter. He's Sheldon's personal bodyguard. He's in charge of security on the *Cocoa Bean*."

"I'm not sure if that is good news or bad news. If Sheldon needs a bodyguard, that means he expects trouble," Dawn said disturbed by the news.

"Sheldon doesn't expect trouble, but he wants to be prepared. Rich Americans sailing in the Mediterranean would be a prime target for some terrorist group."

"And you expect Franklin to stop a terrorist attack?" Dawn was getting a little nervous being aboard the *Cocoa Bean*.

"He's not alone you know. Relax, Dawn, you're in very good hands."

"Okay. If you say so. Would you like a sip of my Fuzzy Navel?"

"No thanks. I'll wait for the real thing."

"It may be a long wait," Dawn teased.

"But it may not," Howard replied. "Remember, you're with a pro tonight. I buy and sell the future every day. Right now, I'd say our future is a buy."

They leaned on the railing watching Cannes slowly disappear from view. The sun was setting in a blaze of glorious color across the western sky.

"Why don't you try cocoa beans Howard? This is such a fabulous ship. Maybe you could strike it rich like Sheldon did."

"I did try cocoa beans," Howard said sadly.

"What happened?"

"Sheldon was right. I was wrong."

"How terrible," Dawn said with genuine concern.

"It was terrible," Howard admitted. "A million dollars terrible!"

"You're kidding."

"I wish I was."

"You mean you lost a million dollars!"

"In one day," Howard added.

"The million dollars Sheldon made in one day was your money?"

"Right on Dawn. That's why I feel so comfortable on the *Cocoa Bean*. I helped pay for it."

"How did you ever come up with a million dollars cash?"

It wasn't easy. A rich uncle bailed me out. We're partners now and luckily I made him more money than he put up to bail me out."

"You sure know how to pick your relatives."

"How about you Dawn? Tell me about yourself."

"Not much to tell. I was born in Los Angeles. My parents divorced when I was little. My Mom raised me as best she could. I got through high school and took a couple of courses at UCLA. Then the money ran out. I started modelling and have been at it ever since. Good pay, boring mostly and you meet some really strange people."

"What is your secret dream Dawn? What would you really like to do if you could afford anything you wanted?"

"You do ask interesting questions Mr. Greenfield. I never gave it much thought. I've always lived a month-to-month existence. I suppose if I had all the money I needed, I'd like to run my own health club. I'm keen on physical fitness. I run, do aerobics, lift weights, the whole thing. I think people should keep in good shape. They'll be healthier, live longer."

"You certainly practice what you preach," Howard said as he stepped back and slowly inspected his dinner companion.

Dawn enjoyed his flirtations. His eyes seemed to hunger for more.

"I hear music," Howard said. "Should we go back and try the dance floor?"

"Wonderful idea." Dawn wanted to feel him press her close to his body. She was feeling so feminine tonight, so eager to show Howard how much she enjoyed his company.

They walked hand in hand down the deck to the main lounge. A five piece orchestra was playing *Stardust*. Several couples were already on the dance floor. Howard and Dawn sat down at a small table. Franklin came promptly.

"May I bring you drinks?"

"Thank you Franklin, that would be fine," Howard replied. Franklin gave the order to the bartender and then stopped at a nearby table to take their order.

The lounge was a gallery of mirrors. It was wonderful for people watching. You could observe what was happening all around you. Suddenly, there was an angry shout.

"No you don't," Franklin yelled. He vaulted over the bar and crashed the bartender against the wall. The orchestra seemed unsure what to do, so *Stardust* continued accented by the sound of broken glass and curses.

Howard jumped up to see if he could help Franklin. Before he reached the bar, the bartender, a slim Frenchman, had slipped out of Franklin's grasp. Franklin was left holding the bartender's jacket. With Franklin, Howard and several guests in hot pursuit, the Frenchman disappeared around the corner of the deck. The next shout Dawn heard was: "Man overboard!"

The ship shuddered to a stop and then slowly circled. Spotlights pierced the darkness and danced frantically across the waves. A lifeboat was lowered, but the Frenchman had vanished.

Sheldon Waxman appeared in the lounge red-faced and nervous.

"I'm so very sorry for this incident," Sheldon told his guests. "Franklin happened to look at a mirror and saw the bartender adding something to a guest's drink. I'm afraid we will have to close the bar and head back to Cannes."

Sheldon came over to Howard and Dawn. "Could you both come with me to my cabin? I'd like to show you something."

Sheldon's cabin was fit for an admiral. It was a large room with a king size bed, stereo equipment, a large TV and an antique teak desk. Sheldon sat down behind the desk and motioned Dawn and Howard to the nearby upholstered chairs.

"Franklin gets overly suspicious sometimes, but tonight he stopped a murder."

"A murder!" Howard exclaimed.

"Oh my God!" Dawn gasped.

Sheldon continued: "The bartender jumped overboard. It's two miles to shore so he'd have to be a very good swimmer to make it. All we have is the bartender's jacket. We found two things in his pockets. Sheldon opened his desk drawer and took out an 8 x 10 photograph that had been folded into a small square.

It was a head shot of Dawn Reynolds. He opened the photograph on his desk.

"What was he doing with my picture?" Dawn was obviously very frightened.

"That's not all we found." Sheldon placed a small glass bottle on his desk. A skull and crossbones covered the front of the bottle. In large print it read: 'Poison–Cyanide.' "The bartender was fixing a Fuzzy Navel when Franklin spotted him taking something out of his pocket to put into Dawn's drink. Two drops of this in your Fuzzy Navel and you would be dead in 30 seconds."

"Why would someone want to kill me? This is crazy!"

"Somehow Dawn, you have acquired some very serious enemies," Sheldon said very distressed about what almost happened to one of his guests.

"I suggest you leave France as soon as possible. Don't trust anyone except Howard. Do not contact the French police. They will keep you here for a long time while they investigate what happened."

Sheldon came around the desk and kissed Dawn goodbye. He clapped Howard on the shoulder. "Good luck to both of you. Be careful, very careful."

Dawn was shivering as she sat in the motor launch headed for the pier. Howard put his arm around her. "Dawn, you're shaking. Take my jacket."

"I'm not cold Howard. I'm scared." Dawn clung to Howard in the darkness and wept in his arms. Why would Wilbur Thompson try to kill her? She had kept her part of the bargain. His secret was safe with her. Why the double cross? Unless, it wasn't Wilbur? Wilbur wasn't a killer. She was sure of that. You get to know a man pretty well when you help him act out his sexual fantasies. She knew a lot more about Wilbur Thompson then his own wife did. But he was part of a group, a bunch of Bible fanatics. Maybe one of the group got nervous about her. Dawn was the only link that could connect their group to the kidnapping of Jenny Sanders. If they would kidnap a young girl, why not murder? Her murder?

Chapter

Twenty-Three

DAWN'S HOTEL ROOM OVERLOOKED the beach. Lights from the ships in the harbor flickered like tiny candles in the wind. It looked so peaceful, yet in the darkness violent men plotted against the innocent and not so innocent.

Dawn came out of the bathroom wearing bikini pajamas. She crawled under the covers. "Howard, close the light and come sit by me."

Howard sat on the edge of the bed and stroked Dawn's silky long hair.

"I am so sorry Howard. I had wonderful ideas about our first night together. I'm just too nervous now."

"I understand. There will be other nights."

"Could I ask you a favor?"

"Sure. What is it?"

"Would you stay with me tonight? I don't want to be alone. I'm really scared. Just lie next to me and hold me."

Howard undressed to his shorts and slipped into bed next to Dawn. She curled in his arms and soon fell into a deep sleep. Nothing like a death threat to unmask a person, Howard thought. From a sophisticated, worldly woman, Dawn Reynolds was like a frightened little girl. She clung to him as she must have held her teddy bear during a thunderstorm when she was a child.

Why would anyone want to kill such a lovely young woman? And why did his favorite uncle, Max Levi, ask him to go to France and persuade Dawn Reynolds to come back to Chicago? Howard didn't know the answers, but he was sure Dawn and Uncle Max did.

Howard drifted off to sleep with the most beautiful woman he ever met lying next to him. He could never tell his friends about this night. Who would believe that Howard Edward Greenfield, Chicago's most reliable lover, could just lie quietly next to a sensuous, nearly nude woman.

In the morning, Howard awoke with a start. Dawn was gone. He heard a man's voice on the balcony. He pulled on his pants and yanked open the bedroom door. To his relief, he saw Dawn and the waiter arranging breakfast trays. The waiter left with a broad smile after pocketing Dawn's overly generous tip.

"Hi sleepyhead." Dawn kissed him lightly on the lips. "Thank you for last night. It's nice to know there are still gentlemen in this world."

"It wasn't easy. I spent most of the night in a cold shower."

"Liar," Dawn laughed. It was a genuine laugh. Dawn looked refreshed and enticing in a daring swimsuit.

"Dawn, you should be the next model for *Sports Illustrated*. You look fabulous."

"Thank you, kind sir." Dawn twirled for his inspection and ended in his arms. They clung to each other feeling the warmth of their bodies melt together.

"Let's eat," Dawn said as she led Howard to the table. It was a beautiful view from the balcony. The sapphire blue sea stretched before them with white sails dotting the horizon.

"That's strange," Howard said as he scanned the harbor. "I don't see the *Cocoa Bean*. Sheldon just scooted off to avoid a long investigation."

With the mention of the *Cocoa Bean,* Dawn's smile vanished. The fright of last night dropped a curtain between them. Howard could feel it and wanted to reach through and grab her, hold her, protect her. He had to know what was going on. What was the secret that Dawn and Uncle Max shared?

"Dawn," he said reaching across the table to hold her hand, "I'll tell you the whole truth if you tell me why that man tried to kill you."

Dawn was silent for a few moments. The truth, the whole truth and nothing but the truth. That's a tough order, Mr. Nice Guy. The truth was that she really liked Howard and once he heard the truth of what she did for a living, he would just vanish from her life. Why would he want a woman with such a wild past? Yet, she knew she was really a good person. She could love a man and be faithful if only he would give her a chance.

"The truth isn't very pretty Howard."

"I'm not your judge Dawn, I'm your friend."

Dawn retrieved her hand and sipped her coffee. "Okay Howard, but you go first."

"Well," Howard began, "it all started a few days ago when I received a phone call from my Uncle Max. He's the rich uncle I told you about who saved my scalp on my cocoa bean fiasco. He also owns 300 Town & Country shops throughout the country. You may have heard of them."

"Everyone has. They're in all the malls. Maybe you can get me a discount."

"I'll check with Uncle Max."

"Don't forget. Shopping is my favorite hobby."

"Uncle Max is really a super guy, a real legend. He started with just one store in Chicago and now controls one of the top retail chains in America. He's involved in all kinds of things besides business. He helped finance the hunt for the hidden Nazis who killed so many Jews and has donated millions to the U.S. Holocaust Museum.

"I'd do anything for him, but he never asked me for anything until last week. When I came to his house, he gave me a photo of you, just like the one the bartender had. He gave me the name of your hotel and told me to ask Andre to introduce me to you. Then he gave me a roundtrip ticket to Cannes and a ticket for you to come back to Chicago.

"He thought you were in serious danger and he needed you to help a friend who was also in danger. That's all he told me. He said I would learn the rest later. He also arranged with an old friend of his, Sheldon Waxman, to anchor the *Cocoa Bean* here for a few days to entertain us. That's the truth, the whole truth. Now, let's hear your story, the real story."

Dawn continued to sip her coffee. It would have been so nice. A life with Howard, rich, fun-loving, gentle Howard. Once he heard about her past, he'd be gone forever.

"I must say, your Uncle Max has quite a spy network. I wonder how he found me?"

"If they could find where Adolf Eichmann was hiding, the manager of the death camps, they can find anyone, anywhere," Howard replied.

"Uncle Max seems to know everything about me except my bra size."

"That I'm sure he knows. That's a big part of his business."

"It's a big part of me also," Dawn smiled.

"Praise the Lord," Howard said enthusiastically.

Now it was Dawn's turn to tell the Truth. What truth? The truth that her father left when she was a baby? That her mother struggled to raise her on her salary as a lingerie saleslady at Macys? That her mother died of lung cancer just after Dawn graduated from high school? That money was always scarce?

Dawn filled her coffee cup from the silver pot the waiter had left. She looked out at the sleek yachts slowly swaying with the waves. That was the way to live. No worries about money. Just sunny, fun-filled days and exciting nights with Howard. But that was a dream. Soon Howard would be gone, just like her Mom and Dad were gone. She would be alone again. All alone.

Dawn looked at the handsome man across the table, a real gentleman. He had slept with her and protected her. Soon he would be ashamed of her.

"It's not a pretty story," Dawn began. "In Los Angeles, models were a dime a dozen. Thousands of beautiful girls flocked to Hollywood looking for an acting career. I decided to make a new start. A girlfriend from high school invited me to come to Chicago where she had moved and stay with her. I took her up on her offer and got a job working as a waitress at Michael Jordan's Steak House on Michigan Avenue in Chicago. The work was hard, but the tips were good. One of the girls I worked with told me how she made some extra money as an escort. She gave me the phone number of Gold Coast Escort Service.

"I called for an appointment and met the owner, Mrs. Rose. She was a dignified middle- aged lady with silver sprinkles in her hair. She took my application and had me photographed.

"Two weeks later, Mrs. Rose called me. She said the Auto Show was in town and she had a client who wanted a young lady to have dinner with him and go dancing. He would pay $1,000 for the evening and I would give half to Mrs. Rose. Mrs. Rose told me sex was not part of the deal. If he wanted sex, it was up to me, but I should charge extra for it.

"I took the appointment and had a good time that night. We had dinner at the Italian Village and then dancing at Studio Paris. I was treated like a lady. I had fun and made good money. Much easier than being a waitress.

"Mrs. Rose kept calling me. Clients asked for me. I quit my job as a waitress. I was making really good money with Mrs. Rose. I thought about going to college to study for some career, but frankly I was having fun and making too much money to quit. I became addicted.

"I liked going to fancy restaurants, being with men who had power and money, shopping on Oak Street instead of at the malls. Instead of college, I was getting a graduate course in sex education. Some of the big, powerful men who were tigers on the job would be little pussycats in bed with me. Some wanted me to spank them like they were bad little boys. Some of the quiet, serious executives would act out their wild fantasies with me. Whatever they wanted, I gave them, for a price.

"I was with Mrs. Rose for three years. What used to be fun was getting boring. Pleasing men's fantasies was certainly profitable, but after a while it became routine and sometimes disgusting. I was giving pleasure, but I wasn't getting any. I was with a man almost every night, but I had no man of my own. I was still alone. I made love to strangers, but there was no love in my life.

"I decided to quit and start a new life. Maybe college, maybe a business career. I wasn't sure. That's when a regular client called me and asked me to have dinner with him. He had a business proposition for me."

Dawn paused and got up from the table. She stood by the railing and watched couples walk hand in hand on the beach below. Howard came and put his arms around her waist.

"All that is in the past Dawn. You have your whole life ahead of you."

"Judging from last night, it may be a very short life. I can't believe someone really tried to kill me."

"Who Dawn? Who tried to kill you and why?"

Dawn returned to the table and resumed her story.

"My client told me about a book that was about to be published that said awful things about the Bible. He and his organization wanted to stop the publication of that slanderous book. I'm not a religious person, but I could understand someone trying to protect the Bible.

"He described his plan where I would help him pick up the young daughter of the author. We would take her to his home in Indianapolis where he and his wife would treat her like a guest. They just wanted to scare the author so he would promise not to publish his book. He swore to me that the young girl would not be hurt in anyway.

"I had known this man for years. I slept with him probably once a month when he came to Chicago on business, or maybe I was his business. I wasn't sure. He was a kind, generous person. Sometimes, a little kinky."

"What does that mean?" Howard interrupted.

"Well, he was a very religious man. He would read all kinds of lurid novels and non-fiction books like Nancy

Friday's *Women on Top* to see if they should be banned from the libraries. He wanted to protect the public from dangerous literature. But some of the ideas intrigued him so much, he wanted to try them with me."

"For example," Howard persisted.

"He was fascinated with bondage. He would lie down on the bed and give me his outstretched arms to tie to the bedposts. I was a girl scout so I knew how to tie a square knot that would never come loose. Then I would sit on his chest and tell him he was my prisoner and was going to be my sex slave. He would beg me to let him go and struggled hard to free himself. When he was squirming beneath me, I would slap his face and order him to lie still.

"I threatened to smother him with a pillow if he didn't do exactly what I demanded. It was a game he liked to play and to tell the truth, I liked it too. I was in charge. I was the boss. I had a big, rich business executive tied naked helpless beneath me. He was at my mercy. I could do anything I wanted to him and he couldn't stop me. I could kill him and he knew it and I knew it.

"After I tormented him and he was practically crying with frustration, I would take him inside of me and he would explode like a gunshot. He told me it was the greatest orgasm he ever had.

"He trusted me not to hurt him. And I trusted him not to hurt me when I did untie him even though I had given him some pretty hard slaps.

"Like I said, I had decided to quit the sex business so when he offered me $100,000 cash to help him with the young girl, I figured this was my big chance to start a new life. No one would get hurt. What harm would it do? There would just be one less book to gather dust on some library shelf. From the sex games we had played, he knew he could trust me with his secrets just as he had trusted me with his life and I trusted him to keep his promise not to hurt the girl.

"After I dropped him and Jenny off at his house, I was to take the van back to Chicago, wipe the van clean so there would be no fingerprints and leave the van at the O'Hare Airport parking lot. That's what I did and then I took the "L" back to the city.

"He told me never to mention his name and just disappear out of the country for a year or so until all the fuss about the kidnapping died down. I did everything he asked, so why did someone from his group try to kill me?"

"I don't know Dawn, but I know you will be safe with me. My job is to get you back to Chicago where we can protect you. When can you be ready to leave?"

"I'm not going back with you Howard, much as I would really love to."

"You've got to be kidding. You want to sit around here until they try again?"

"They can kill me in Chicago too."

"But we have people to protect you."

"Forever? Will they protect me forever Howard or just until dear Uncle Max gets what he wants from me?"

"Dawn, I'm sure we could protect you. It would be far better than you being alone."

"I won't be alone Howard. I won't be at all. Dawn Reynolds is going to vanish off the face of the earth. I didn't expect someone to come looking for me in France so I didn't try to hide my identity. Now I will. I'll get false documents, cut my hair, change its color. I'll dress differently, talk differently. I can go anywhere. Back to the States, London, Australia, Japan, Israel. It's a big world. If you have money, you can disappear in the crowd. I have money Howard and I've decided the only way to really be safe is just to vanish.

"Give my apologies to Uncle Max. I'd really like to help him, but I just can't. I plan to be a survivor, not a hero. Tell that to Uncle Max. He'll understand. He's a survivor. The heroes of the Holocaust were all killed."

"Please reconsider, I don't want to lose you." Howard said desperately.

"We just met Howard. We hardly know one another. Look for another girl on the beach without so much baggage. You are a great guy Howard and I would have loved to get to know you better. But I'm a target now and I have to protect myself the best way I know how."

They embraced on the balcony and kissed goodbye. "Good luck Dawn. I will really miss you."

"I'll miss you too Howard, more than you will ever know."

After Howard left, Dawn threw herself on the bed and wept for the life she would be leaving behind.

Chapter

Twenty-Four

TEARS STREAMED DOWN HOWARD'S cheeks as he reread the letter for the third time.

"Dear Howard,

Since I left you in France, I have thought about you constantly. My dream of happiness is to be with you always. Sadly this cannot be.

Even if you could forgive my sinful past, I could never forgive myself. What I did to Jenny and her parents was inexcusable. I have decided to end this life of fear, worry, loneliness and regrets. Perhaps my next life will be better.

Enclosed with this letter is a video with my full confession.

Call the police department on Staten Island and report my suicide. I am leaving the hotel now to go to the marina on Staten Island where I have reserved a small sailboat. I will sail out a few miles and then go for a swim. The water will be very cold. I will swim as long as I can. It will all be over soon.

I do love you. Dawn"

Howard picked up the phone and called the Staten Island Police Department. "I want to report a suicide," he told the operator. She connected him to Detective Peter Leonardo.

"My name is Howard Edward Greenfield of Chicago. I received a suicide letter this morning from Dawn Reynolds."

"I already know about it Mr. Greenfield. I was about to call you."

"How did you know?"

"We had a call late yesterday afternoon from the Marina. They reported a sailboat was three hours overdue. We notified the Coast Guard. They sent a helicopter to check the area. The pilot spotted the boat drifting about five miles offshore. There was no sign of an occupant. The Coast Guard towed the boat back to the Marina. One of our officers went there to collect any personal effects."

"What did he find?" Howard asked holding back his tears. "Could you give me all the details?"

"Certainly. Let me get the report. There was only one large grey handbag with a shoulder strap. Inside the bag was a passport with a photo of a blonde woman named Dawn Reynolds. There was a beige wallet with a driver's license, Visa card, American Express card and $140.00 in cash. There was also a note addressed 'To Whom It May Concern.'"

"What did the note say?" Howard asked impatiently.

"I have it right here," the detective replied. "It is written in longhand. Nice handwriting too. The note says: 'My name is Dawn Reynolds. It hurts too much to go on living. Please contact Mr. Howard Edward Greenfield of Glencoe, Illinois. All my belongings are to go to him. When my body washes ashore, I'm sure he will arrange for the burial.'"

"Oh my God. You stupid, stupid girl!" Howard sobbed quietly.

"One other curious thing we found Mr. Greenfield."

"What's that?"

"There was a bar card enclosed with the suicide note."

"What's a bar card?"

"It's a recipe for a drink. Guess what drink is on that card?"

"I have no idea," Howard lied.

"It's for a Fuzzy Navel. Weird name. I never heard of it before. Have you?"

"No. I never heard of it," Howard smiled with tears in his eyes. "Anything else detective?"

"That's it. Sorry about your friend. The Marina attendant said she was a beautiful woman."

"She was detective. She really was. Thank you for your help."

Chapter

Twenty-Five

THEY HAD ALL ASSEMBLED in Max Levi's large entertainment room. Everyone connected with *The Trial of St. John* had come to watch the video Dawn had sent Howard.

"Now that everyone is here, let's get started." Max motioned to Adam Vogel to play the video on the large screen TV.

"My name is Dawn Reynolds. I participated in the kidnapping of Jenny Sanders. Please forgive me Jenny and Mr. and Mrs. Sanders. It was a terrible thing to do, but I knew that Jenny would not be hurt. I did it for the money. I thought the $100,000 paid me would help me start a new life."

"That's her Mom!" Jenny said excitedly. "That's the lady who drove the van except she wasn't blonde then."

Adam pressed the pause button.

"Are you sure, Jenny?" Max asked.

"I'm positive," Jenny insisted.

"Did the lady ever hurt you Jenny?" Sandra Price asked from a rocking chair in the corner of the room.

"No. She tried to be real nice, but I was still scared."

"Of course you were," Sandra said in a soothing voice.

Michael Morris noted Sandra's soft side. He had only known her as the wise-cracking, flirtatious, tough lady who used to own Harborside Press.

"OK Adam, let's continue," Max instructed.

Dawn's beautiful face came back on the screen. Her golden hair had a halo around it from the back light she was using for the video. It gave her the look of an angel. Howard fought to hold back the tears as he looked into the mysterious green eyes of the woman who captured his heart that magical night in Cannes.

Dawn was speaking: "The money did not buy me anything but trouble. Someone tried to kill me. I was so scared I left the one man I thought I could really love. I'm tired of hiding. Tired of being lonely. I'm going to save the kidnappers the trouble. When you play this, I will be dead. No more fears. No more running. The money I had left I put into an account at Citibank in London for Jenny. Use it for college Jenny and try to think of me sometime as a nice lady who somehow managed to screw up her life."

Howard could feel the tears streaming down his face.

"The man who paid me $100,000 to help him kidnap Jenny is Wilbur Thompson. He and his wife Martha live at 367 Arbor Lane in Indianapolis. He owns Thompson

Cadillac and has several showrooms in the Indianapolis area.

"They used disguises and false names during the kidnapping, but I assure you it was the Thompsons. If necessary, Jenny could identify the rooms she saw in the house.

"I knew Mr. Thompson for three years. I was his girlfriend for pay whenever he came to Chicago which was about once a month. My agent, Mrs. Rose of Gold Coast Escort Service, can verify the facts for you.

"Mr. Thompson was always nice to me, but he was a fanatic about the Bible. He promised me that Jenny would not be hurt and thank heavens she was not. However, he and his organization might not be so gentle the next time.

"I never really believed in God. But now I hope there is one. I hope there is another life so I can have another chance. Goodbye Howard. I'm sorry we didn't have more time to really get to know one another. I think you could have learned to like me. I know I could have loved you forever.

"Please forgive me everyone."

The screen went black. "Stupid girl," Max said bitterly, "she didn't have to kill herself. We could have taken care of her."

"I know Uncle Max. I tried my best to convince her to come home with me. I should never have let her go." Howard felt the guilt stab at his heart.

"Not your fault Howard," Max replied. "Dawn was a grown woman. She had the right to make her own decisions about her life. Terribly sad she made the wrong choice. Life is too precious to be destroyed. But what is done is done. Now we have to decide what to do with this video. First, let's go into the dining room for some snacks while we talk about it."

As they filed into the dining room, Michelle took Howard aside.

"Howard, you never told me that Max Levi was your uncle."

"I'm afraid I kept a few things from you," Howard confessed.

"What else for heaven's sake?"

"It's about my new house."

"Oh Howard, don't tell me the roof leaks and the toilets don't flush. I pleaded with you to check the house before buying it," Michelle said with genuine concern.

"No. The house is just fine. But I was teasing you about not wanting to see the inside. I didn't have to see the inside because I practically grew up in that house."

"You're kidding. You mean you're not an eccentric millionaire after all?"

"Not when it comes to spending big bucks," Howard smiled. "That was the Gordon home. Andy Gordon and I were best friends in high school. His folks were killed in a terrible auto accident on Interstate 294 last year. Andy called me from California to let me know the trustees would be putting his old house on the market. I'm glad you got the listing."

"You're glad. I was ecstatic. Thanks for telling me the whole story. I'm really sorry about Dawn. I can tell you really cared for her."

"Thanks Michelle."

In the corner of the large dining room, Sandra Price and Max Levi were engaged in an earnest conversation.

"I don't understand Max why you don't give the video to the FBI. Let the Thompsons rot in jail. They deserve it."

"Of course they deserve it Sandra, but putting them in jail won't solve our problem. What if other members of their group decide to carry out the threat to kill Jenny if you publish *The Trial of St. John*?"

"So how can we stop them? Or do we just let Ben's book die?"

"Believe me Sandra, I want Ben's book published as much as you do. But first, we must remove the threat hanging over the Sanders family."

"I agree Max. But how? What's the answer?"

"The answer is first to ask the right questions," Max replied with a faint smile.

Sandra was not amused. "Max Levi, stop talking in riddles. Let's get down to business."

Max laughed out loud. He couldn't remember the last time he laughed.

"What's so funny?" Sandra asked her famous host.

"Sandra Price, you are true to your reputation. Michael warned me about you."

"What did that whipper-snapper say?" Sandra was enjoying their verbal bout.

"He said you were a tough old broad who wouldn't take doubletalk from anyone, even me."

"Did he also tell you that I was an outrageous flirt who kept trying to seduce him?"

"No. He didn't tell me that, but I wish he had."

"Why Mr. Levi, I do believe there is hope for you yet."

"Now what does that mean, young lady," Max replied with mock seriousness.

"That means you should be ashamed of yourself hiding away in this beautiful mansion all by yourself."

"My work keeps me busy."

"I know it does. And you do wonderful work Max, but what makes you happy? Who is your soulmate?"

"I haven't thought about it."

"Maybe you should Max. Maybe you should."

"Perhaps I will someday. After we get Ben's book published, would you join me for lunch and we can explore our souls together?"

"I'd love to," Sandra smiled triumphantly. "Now, what's the plan? How am I going to get Ben's book published?"

Max Levi laughed again. He gathered the group around him and explained why he would not give the video to the FBI.

Chapter

Twenty-Six

WILBUR THOMPSON WAS IN his office at Thompson Cadillac. The sales figures were excellent. The charts on his desk showed all five showrooms ahead of last year. Too bad about Dawn. He had read about her suicide in the *New York Times*. He couldn't understand why she would kill herself. Everything had gone according to plan. No one was hurt. She got her money. The book was dead. Why in the world would such a lovely young lady kill herself?

He would miss her. Dawn was so much fun. So eager to please him. Of course, he loved his wife, but he couldn't play games with her like he did with Dawn. Dawn understood him. He was a man. He had desires. The Devil is in all of us, in the flesh, in the body. Sometimes he just couldn't resist.

In Indianapolis, he was a pillar of the community, a Church leader. In Chicago, he was free, free of all his

184

inhibitions. With Dawn, he felt like a wild buck again. He was fighting the clock. Time was rushing by. He was 56 years old. How many years did he have left? How long would he even have desires for sex and play? Why did she kill herself? What terrible pain did she suffer? Wilbur didn't understand. He couldn't understand because he did not know someone had tried to murder Dawn.

Wilbur's phone buzzed.

"Long distance for you, Mr. Thompson."

"Who is it?"

"He wouldn't say. Said it was personal."

"All right. Put him through." Wilbur was annoyed. Probably another pitch for a charitable donation. He was on everyone's list. "This is Wilbur Thompson."

"Mr. Thompson, my name is Max Levi from Chicago."

"What can I do for you Mr. Levi?"

Wilbur thought the name was familiar, but couldn't place it. Jewish name, serious voice.

"I have something important to show you Mr. Thompson. I think you should come to Chicago so I can show you in private."

"Why in hell should I come to Chicago to meet you Mr. Levi? I don't even know you."

"But you knew Dawn Reynolds. I have a video she made before she died. It has to do with you and the kidnapping of Jenny Sanders."

"Damn that bitch. How could she do that to me after all I did for her. Okay Mr. Levi, where shall we meet?"

"Be at the Four Seasons tomorrow at 5 PM. Same suite you always had with Dawn."

"Okay. I'll be there."

"And Mr. Thompson."

"Yes?"

"Bring your checkbook."

Adam Vogel and Max Levi were in the suite when Wilbur Thompson arrived. Adam had his 45 Colt in his chest holster, but he didn't expect to need it. The men introduced themselves. No one shook hands.

Max said: "Mr. Thompson, this is a copy of the video Dawn made. The original is in my vault at the Chase Bank in case this copy gets lost. Adam, play the video."

The men sat quietly while Dawn talked to them from the large TV screen. When the video was finished, Wilbur said: "That poor girl. I don't know where she got the idea I tried to have her killed. I never had anything to do with that. I never hurt anyone in my life Mr. Levi. I am a devout Christian."

"I've seen devout Christians in action Mr. Thompson. It was not a pretty sight," Max said. "But you did threaten to kill Jenny if *The Trial of St. John* was ever published."

"That was just a bluff to scare them. I would never do such a terrible thing."

"I believe you Mr. Thompson," Adam Vogel said in his deep Hungarian accent, "but can you be sure others in your group would not kill for a noble cause, to save the Bible?"

"I don't know what others might do Mr. Vogel. I only know that I would not hurt anyone."

"Who else knows you were involved in the kidnapping?" Max asked.

"The only other person who knows is the Reverend Paul Henry Porter of Memphis, the TV preacher."

"Did he help you plan the kidnapping?" Max continued.

"Of course not. My wife and I told him about it afterwards in strict confidence."

"Why did you tell him?" Adam asked.

"So he could use his TV sermons to protect the Gospels against the disrespect shown by Professor Sanders.

"Now I'd like to ask you something Mr. Levi. Why am I here? Why didn't you just give the video to the FBI? Are you blackmailers?"

"Of course we are Mr. Thompson. It takes one to know one."

"How much do you want for the video?"

"How much is it worth to keep you and your wife from spending the rest of your life in prison?" Max asked.

"Everything." Wilbur replied softly.

"That should be enough. Here is what you must do immediately."

Max handed Wilbur a typed list of instructions.

Wilbur Thompson flew back to Indianapolis that evening. His fortune would be seriously diminished, but he was free. The Jews were tough, very tough, but jail would have been worse, unthinkable.

Chapter

Twenty-Seven

CHARLOTTE GREEN OPENED THE morning mail. Hopefully, some checks would be there to help them reach their goal. She held an envelope in her hand and looked at the return address.

"How strange? I wonder what he wants?" she mused to herself. She slit the envelope and held a blue business check in her hand. Charlotte rushed from her desk into the office of Nathan Goldberg, Executive Director of the Indiana United Jewish Fund.

"Look at this! Do you think it is some kind of prank?"

Mr. Goldberg took the check and studied it carefully.

"Wilbur Thompson is giving us one million dollars! I wonder why? I'll call him and make sure this is legit."

Nathan dialed the number for the main showroom of Thompson Cadillac and was promptly connected. "Mr. Thompson, this is Nathan Goldberg from the United Jewish Fund. I called to thank you for your very generous donation."

"My pleasure, Mr. Goldberg. I just wanted to give something to the community that has been very good to me over the years. You know, we have many Jewish customers at Thompson Cadillac. Hopefully, we may have even more in the future."

"I'm sure your generosity will be noticed. In fact, if you would send me a glossy photograph we'll print it in our next newsletter with a story about your very generous donation."

"I'll send it to you today."

"Thank you again Mr. Thompson. We really do appreciate your generous donation."

"I'm glad I could help with the wonderful work that you do." Wilbur Thompson crossed off number one from the list given to him by Max Levi.

At the United States Holocaust Memorial Museum in Washington, D.C., the gift from Wilbur Thompson was one million dollars. A bronze plaque with his name would be placed on the wall leading to the Auschwitz exhibit.

The Simon Wiesenthal Center in Los Angeles also received a gift of one million dollars from the very generous Wilbur Thompson.

The final item on the list of instructions from Max Levi was the letter sent by Wilbur Thompson to all members of the Christian Alliance.

"Dear Friends,

To advance the cause of Christian Brotherhood, we must carry into our lives the message of Jesus: 'Love thy neighbor as thyself.' This means all our neighbors: Blacks and Whites, Jews and Gentiles.

Our organization will not condone or tolerate any acts of violence, even against those who oppose our views.

Yours in faith,
Wilbur Thompson, Chairman"

Chapter

Twenty-Eight

SANDRA PRICE HAD NEVER been to Memphis. She had been to Birmingham where she marched with Dr. Martin Luther King, Jr. The South was like a foreign country in those days. Separate drinking fountains and toilets. Negroes, as they were called then if you were being polite, had to sit in the back of the buses. Signs everywhere: "No Coloreds Allowed Here." It was like Germany in the 1930's, before the death camps. No Jews allowed in this town, or in this store or on this job.

How can civilized people be so stupid? Sandra knew the answer. Richard Rogers and Oscar Hammerstein II said it best in *South Pacific*: "You had to be to taught to hate."

Sandra took a cab from the airport to the Gospel Church. A pleasant lady ushered her into Reverend Paul Henry Porter's large study. Paul Henry rose to greet his visitor. She was not as young as he expected from her phone call. Petite, silver hair, tailored suit, soft features, an attractive woman.

"You had a pleasant trip I trust," the Reverend said as he shook hands with the little Jewish lady. He motioned her to a comfortable armchair as he went back to his desk. "On the phone, you mentioned you had a package for me from Wilbur Thompson."

"Here it is Reverend," Sandra said as she slid a copy of Dawn's video across the desk. "When you have time to play the video, you'll see it is a suicide confession from a woman named Dawn Reynolds."

"I'm afraid I don't recall that name."

"She was the lady who helped kidnap the young girl Mr. and Mrs. Thompson told you about."

"I see." The Reverend studied Sandra Price. What was this all about, he wondered.

"You know Mrs. Price, I was told that information in priestly confidence. I could not go to the police without breaking my oath."

"I understand Reverend. You have done nothing wrong."

"Then why have you come to see me?"

"Reverend, I'm the owner of L'Chaim Publishing Company. I have a manuscript from Professor Benjamin Sanders, *The Trial of St. John,* which I hope to send to the printers very soon."

"That name I know Mrs. Price. I assume you also know that I strongly disapprove of his views."

"That is certainly your right sir. I came to explain some of the background of the book you are not aware of."

"I'm listening." The lady came all this way. He would give her the courtesy of a hearing. But nothing was going to change his mind. Professor Sanders has written a very dangerous book.

"First, let me explain how Professor Sanders came to write his book."

Sandra told how Jenny Sanders had been brutalized and terrorized by four young hoodlums who tied her to a cross of Jesus and stripped her naked. She also told how Jenny was rescued by Father Dominick.

"That is outrageous," Paul Henry said, genuinely shocked and saddened. "Are you suggesting the Holy Bible is to blame because four boys did not understand the message of love that is the heart and soul of Christianity? If Jews commit some crime, we don't blame Judaism for their crime. Why should Professor Sanders blame the Bible if some Christians do not practice their faith as taught by Jesus Christ? Those boys were at fault, not their religion."

"There is a difference, Reverend."

"And what is that?"

"Judaism doesn't teach Jews to be criminals. But the Gospels do preach anti-Semitism. You know it is there."

"Yes, it is there. But that is certainly not the essence of the New Testament. Those few remarks should not be taken out of context. The message of the Gospels is the teachings of Jesus."

"I agree Reverend, but tell me this: Do you believe Jesus would have approved of the anti-Jewish comments in the Bible?"

"Certainly not," Paul Henry replied. "But they are there and there is nothing we can do about them now, except ignore them. In fact Mrs. Price, Professor Sander's book could be counterproductive. It might create more anti-Semitism by calling attention to those Biblical passages."

"That is a danger Reverend and that is why I came to see you."

"What can I do about it?"

"Reverend, your TV broadcasts have a nationwide audience. Your opinions influence millions of listeners."

"I know that Mrs. Price. I am very careful about what I say."

"I'm certain you are Reverend, but you may not be aware how your sermons affect some people."

"Meaning what?"

"That video I brought you Reverend, do you know why Dawn Reynolds killed herself?"

"Of course not. Why did she?"

"Because someone tried to murder her. Dawn thought that someone connected with the Christian Alliance tried to kill her because she was the only connection to Wilbur Thompson and the kidnapping of Jenny Sanders. Apparently, someone was so desperate to stop the *Trial of St. John* from being published that they wanted to kill Dawn to prevent any criticism of the Gospels."

"That person was totally misguided. I have never preached violence in my life. I abhor violence. I saw enough of it in Vietnam."

"I know that Reverend. Your reputation as a patriot and as a good Christian is beyond reproach. I came to ask you a favor."

"What might that be?"

"When *The Trial of St. John* is in the bookstores, you will probably denounce it in one of your sermons."

"Most likely I will," the Reverend agreed.

"All I ask, in the name of fair play, is that you also tell your listeners that your criticism must not be used as an excuse for violence. Tell your listeners not to buy the book, but tell them also the battle is to be fought with words and ideas, not with stones or bullets."

"That is a reasonable request Mrs. Price. I have no problem preaching against violence. It is one of my major themes. Now, let me ask you a question?"

"Certainly."

"I didn't go to the police because I took an oath not to violate the confidences of the Thompsons. Why haven't you gone to the police?"

"We did consider that Reverend. We could have had the Thompsons locked up for the rest of their lives. But what good would that have done? We knew the Thompsons were not violent people. We decided to impose our own sentence and let Mr. Thompson choose which he preferred."

"You blackmailed him," the Reverend smiled.

"Yes. We blackmailed him to contribute to worthy causes."

"You are obstructing justice you know," Paul Henry chided her. "It seems we are allies in keeping the Thompsons out of jail."

"I hope we can be allies again Reverend for many good causes."

"I don't see why not. I believe our goals are the same. We may just be travelling different paths to reach them."

Sandra got up from her chair. Paul Henry Porter escorted her to the door.

"Thank you for your time Reverend. I do appreciate your seeing me."

"It was a pleasure meeting you Mrs. Price. Have a safe trip home."

Chapter

Twenty-Nine

Now it was up to the Sanders family. Should *The Trial of St. John* be published or was it still too dangerous? Ben Sanders looked at his daughter. God, she was beautiful. A young blossom of womanhood filled with energy, ambition and sweetness. He would rather bury his book than risk any harm to Jenny. She had suffered enough already.

Michelle was sitting next to Ben on the den couch. Jenny was on the floor playing with Dutchess. Michelle loved this room, this family. This was her life. Outside the autumn winds had blown most of the leaves off the old maple tree. Some still clung to life. Their rainbow colors a tribute to the Master Artist.

"I'm still not sure we should go ahead," Ben said.

"Why not Daddy?" Jenny climbed on his lap as she did when she was a little girl. How much longer would she be Daddy's little girl? In a few years, off to college and then a wedding. He would give to another man his most precious daughter. Except for visits now and then, Jenny would be gone. Like a shooting star that lit up his life and then disappeared into a new life of her own. But now, she was his. His to care for, to protect, to shield from danger.

Wilbur Thompson said he was bluffing. He never intended to hurt anyone. How could Ben be sure about other religious fanatics? *The Trial of St. John* was a lightning rod. It could attract trouble, serious trouble. Ben wasn't worried about himself, but how about Michelle and Jenny?

"I'm not afraid Daddy. I want you to publish your book." Jenny put her arms around his neck and gave him a big hug.

"I don't know what else can be done," Michelle said quietly. "Max Levi certainly took care of Mr. Thompson. He won't be a problem anymore. And Sandra was satisfied with her visit with Reverend Porter. What else can we do?"

"We still don't have to print it. I haven't given Sandra the final Okay yet."

"But Daddy, this is America. We are supposed to be free. Free to think, to write, to publish. What if everyone was afraid to voice their true feelings? What kind of country would this be? We would be letting the nuts run the country. I want to go to the library and ask for my Daddy's book. I'm so proud of you professor. Don't you dare disappoint me. Just do it. Do it now!" Jenny ran and brought Ben the phone.

"What do you think Michelle?"

"I think Jenny's right. We can't live our lives worrying about the crazies out there. People get shot everyday just minding their own business, sitting at McDonalds, walking down the street. There are no guarantees in life. We just have to do what is right and pray lightning does not strike us or our loved ones."

"What's the number Daddy?" Jenny insisted. She had become an efficient secretary. "Mrs. Price, please. Professor Sanders is calling." After a moment, "Hi Mrs. Price. It's Jenny. My Dad has something important to tell you."

Ben took the phone. "Well Sandra, the family took a vote. It was unanimous: Print it."

Chapter

Thirty

Ben sat in his office waiting for his next appointment. He smiled to himself as he recalled Jenny's words during their family meeting yesterday: "I'm proud of you professor. Don't you dare disappoint me."

How proud would his daughter be if she saw him handcuffed naked to a bed with the vibrant Cindy Cunningham sitting on top of him? He would be completely helpless to resist Cindy and loving every minute of it. Would his daughter ever understand how a decent man could succumb to raw sexual desires? What would it be like to experience the wild moments he so glibly wrote about in his novels?

"Come in," Ben called in answer to the knock on his door. Cindy closed the door behind her.

"Hi professor," Cindy smiled seductively, "You wanted to see me?"

Cindy was wearing her pink cashmere v-neck pullover. The soft knit accented her full, high breasts. Her long blonde hair framed her delicate features and her smoky blue eyes.

"Please sit down Cindy."

Cindy crossed her legs showing off her naked thighs. "Did you like my paper on Pope John XII and his decisions regarding Hitler?"

"Your paper was excellent, as usual Cindy." Ben pushed the term paper across his desk so Cindy could see the large 'A' on top of the paper.

"Thank you, professor. Is there anything else?" she asked with an eager smile.

"Yes Cindy there is. I think we should talk about the package you sent me."

"I just wanted to be helpful professor. If you write about bondage, I thought you might like to experience it."

"It was a very generous offer. And it was kind of you to be interested in my research. I thank you for that. Would you really want to do such a thing?"

"Why not? It's no big deal really."

"You don't think so?"

"Come on professor. This is the 21st Century. Sex is just a game now. Middle school kids go at it like crazy."

"Do you think it is a good idea?"

"Of course not. They're stupid. They don't know how to protect themselves from getting pregnant."

"And you do?"

"Are you kidding? I have my Trojans with me all the time."

"You know Cindy, they are not foolproof."

"Nothing is perfect professor. Chances are pretty slim that something would go wrong. Why should I miss out on all the fun?"

"It won't be much fun if you get HIV. You should listen to the dying patients who never thought it could happen to them. You could pay a very high price for having some fun."

"Professor, sounds like you are giving me a lecture."

"Cindy, I like you. You are a smart, beautiful young woman. After graduation, you could be successful in any career you chose. But Cindy, you are playing a very dangerous game. You could ruin your life trying to have a little fun now. Your luck could run out."

Ben reached into his bottom drawer and took out the box with the handcuffs inside. He slid the box across his desk.

"Thank you for the offer Cindy. I think it would be a very bad idea for both of us."

"You're the boss professor. I'll think about what you said."

"One more thing Cindy."

"Yes?"

"No more miniskirts in the front row. Even professors are human."

Cindy laughed. "It's a deal. I promise to be good."

Cindy closed the door. Ben looked out his window at the restless lake. His midlife crisis was over, at least for now.

---- ·⊰⊱· ----

Chapter

Thirty-One

THE RUMOR IN THE trading room was that Howard Edward Greenfield had lost his touch. His moves were hesitant, unsure, cautious. In a world of predators, the weak are destroyed. Howard was losing money steadily in his trades. His fortune was slipping through his fingers. Finally, he stopped going to work.

A young trader from the back row took over Howard's old desk. The players change, but the game goes on. New wealth is created from the dust of broken dreams.

Howard had lost more than money. He lost his zest for life. He was not mourning Dawn Reynolds, he was angry at her. How dare she leave him? True, he only knew her for a brief moment in time, but how incredible they were together. It was the promise of an exciting future she took from him.

Now he was home, protected from the monsters that would destroy his wealth, but how could he fill the emptiness in his heart? He tried booze. It just made him sick. He tried women. They made him sicker. Sick of the silly games they played. The fake sophistication, the triumphal surrender to his sexual charms, the lust for his money and for his name.

It was a November morning. Howard sat in the large family room overlooking the waves crashing on the boulders beneath. The dismal clouds and churning waves matched his mood. The quiet was shattered by the ring of the phone.

"Hello," Howard answered listlessly.

"Mr. Greenfield?" inquired a sultry voice tinged with an English accent.

"Yes?"

"My name is Victoria Reed." Oh God, thought Howard. Why don't the girls just leave me alone? "I have a package for you from Dawn Reynolds."

"From Dawn?" Howard was suspicious and excited. "Where did you get it?"

"It's a long story Mr. Greenfield. I promised I would deliver it personally. May I bring it to your home today? Then I will answer all of your questions."

"Certainly. When can you get here?"

"I'm at O'Hare Airport. As soon as I get my luggage, I'll take a taxi."

"Fine. I'll be waiting for you." A package from Dawn? What in Heaven's name could be in a package from Dawn? And who was Victoria Reed? Howard felt a glimmer of excitement. He went up to shower and shave and anoint himself with Brut. He wanted to be presentable for Victoria Reed, his last link to Dawn.

A Yellow Cab pulled into his driveway. A tall brunette stepped out like an English princess. She wore a flowing navy cape trimmed with luxurious fox.

"You must be Victoria."

"In person," she smiled, a warm infectious smile.

Howard took her cape and suitcase and led her to the family room. Her red knit dress caressed every curve of her body. Howard was pleased when Victoria declined a drink so they could get right down to business.

Victoria walked to the huge picture window where she could see the endless expanse of Lake Michigan and also see the glass domed swimming pool.

"Breathtaking," she said with genuine appreciation.

"I'm glad you like it," Howard replied impatiently.

Victoria walked across the room to retrieve the purse she left on the table. She took out a small box and handed it to Howard. Howard carefully undid the gift paper and opened the box. The note said:

"Dear Howard,

Victoria Reed is my cousin. Please be nice to her. She recently lost a loved one. In case you are wondering what's in the box, it's a cocoa bean.

Love, Dawn"

"Your cousin had a strange sense of humor," Howard said passing the note to Victoria.

"I'm sorry Mr. Greenfield, I had no idea what was in the box or the note. I have no wish to intrude on you." Victoria stood up to leave. Could you please call me a taxi?"

"Victoria, please stay. At least tell me about you and Dawn. And for Heaven's sake, stop calling me Mr. Greenfield. Makes me feel like your grandfather."

"OK Howard. Where should I start?"

"In the kitchen. I'm starved. How about you?"

"I thought you would never ask."

What does a millionaire bachelor have in his cupboard? Not much. They dined on Progresso beef vegetable soup, peanut butter and jelly sandwiches and a tossed salad Victoria whipped together using everything she could find including hard boiled eggs and apple slices.

"Not exactly the Ritz, but I like it," Howard said as he finished his lunch with milk and cookies just as he had in high school.

"A good meal is one with good company. The food is incidental," Victoria said, pleased that Howard had relaxed and stopped treating her like an enemy agent.

"Now that we've satisfied my hunger, let's see if you can satisfy my curiosity." Howard led the way back to the family room where they could watch the waves and one another.

Howard considered Victoria carefully. She was beautiful, a bit taller than Dawn and slightly heavier. Her black hair was cut short with an impudent, youthful flair. Her dark brown eyes looked sorrowful.

"So, how are you related to Dawn?"

"We are first cousins. Our mothers were sisters. Some say we look alike. Do you think so?"

"There is certainly a resemblance," Howard said slowly, absorbing the information.

"I know. Dawn is prettier, was prettier." Our family would visit California occasionally so our mothers could visit and Dawn and I became friends. When I graduated high school, my family moved to London. My father was a computer specialist for ExxonMobil. He just died last month."

"I'm very sorry."

"Me too. I really loved that man. He always treated me like I was his little princess. Anyway, he helped ExxonMobil set up a new computer program for their European offices. Dawn and I kept in touch. Cards at Christmas, occasional phone calls."

"When did you see her last?"

"About six months ago. Dawn called me from France and asked if she could stay with me for a while. It was no problem. I have my own flat near Kensington Gardens."

"So she hid out with you?"

"Yes she did. And all she talked about was Howard Edward Greenfield and what a sweet guy he was."

"Did she tell you about the *Cocoa Bean*?"

"I got the whole story, minute by minute including the part where some slimy Frenchman tried to poison her drink. That's why she left you Howard. She was really scared that the organization associated with the kidnappers was out to kill her."

"Did Dawn ever talk about suicide?" Howard asked.

"She was afraid to go out alone. Whenever we went somewhere, she always wore a wig. I remember one night she said: 'I can't live like this. Always running, always hiding, always scared.' I felt so sorry for her, but there was nothing I could do to quash her fears. Her death was such a waste. Dawn was a beautiful person."

"A stupid waste!" Howard said angrily. "Forgive me. I'm not being a very good host. Would you like to see my home?"

"Love to," Victoria replied.

Howard showed off his home like a proud owner. He explained the workings of his huge marble Roman bath with its jets of steaming water. He lingered over the king size bed which sat on a platform in the master bedroom so he could see the lake from his bed. His enthusiasm was growing. It was nice to have a woman, a really nice woman, to show around his home.

"Let me show you my favorite place." It was a short walk from the house to the giant pool house.

"It's magnificent Howard," Victoria exclaimed with sincere enthusiasm.

"This is the fun part." Howard enjoyed showing off his special toy.

He pushed a button and a portion of the glass dome slid open. The cool November air settled slowly around them. Howard was lonely. It was so nice to have a beautiful woman to talk to, to feel comfortable with. As they stood by the pool, Howard reached for Victoria's hand and pulled her close to him.

"May I kiss you Victoria?"

"I'd like that Howard."

They embraced like long lost lovers. Howard's hand found the back zipper of her red knit dress and he slowly pulled it down. Victoria stepped out of her dress and folded it neatly on the lounge chair. She removed her panties and bra and twirled for his inspection and then dove into the pool.

Howard hurriedly undressed and dove into the water. They embraced in the warm water, fondling one another like magnets drawn together by an invisible, irresistible force.

Victoria climbed the steps out of the pool and stretched out on the lounge chair waiting for Howard. She did not have to wait long. Howard pushed a button on the control panel and the glass dome slid shut cutting off the cool outside air. He fell into Victoria's outstretched arms.

"Dawn never had a cousin Victoria," Howard said sternly.

"How do you know that?"

"You're a lousy liar Dawn Reynolds"

"Dawn is dead. I'm Victoria."

"You had me fooled until I saw you in the pool with your beautiful green eyes."

"Damn! My brown contact lenses must have popped out when I dove into the pool. You spoiled my big acting scene. I was going to confess and surprise you. I've been eating like a pig to gain 10 pounds, I cut my hair, had it dyed, wore higher heels and even practiced an English accent."

"Dawn, I should give you a big spanking for all the pain you caused me with your fake suicide. I was so upset, I couldn't work anymore. How did you get back to shore?"

"I had an inflatable pad and a change of clothing with me in a bag. I also had plenty of cash and my new Victoria Reed driver's license. I found a deserted stretch of beach and just blew up my floating pad. I put on my new clothes, paddled to shore and took the Staten Island ferry back to Manhattan. I took a taxi to my hotel and dumped the inflatable pad and the bag in the hotel trash so the police would have no trace of it."

"You are a very clever and very naughty girl Dawn Reynolds," Howard said seriously.

"I'm really so very sorry Howard, but I had to have Dawn vanish so whoever wanted to kill me would stop looking for me. I want Dawn to stay dead. I want to start a new life. Let's bury the past."

"No problem Dawn, I mean Victoria. I think it is a good idea. Victoria is such a nice old fashion name. I like it."

"I like it too. It was my grandmother's name."

From bed, they could see the lake. The waves were no longer angry. Just the rhythmic to and fro of the water beating time against the shore. Relentless time, the ultimate enemy. But for Howard and Victoria, their time was now and they enjoyed it lustfully, eagerly, joyfully.

"I'm going to miss Dawn," Howard said wistfully. "From what she told me, she was quite a wild lady."

"I taught her everything she knew," Victoria insisted.

"You lie," Howard laughed.

"I'll prove it Mr. Greenfield. Turn over on your back," Victoria commanded.

Howard obeyed and Victoria proved it.

Chapter

Thirty-Two

DAWN REYNOLDS LOVED HER new life. As Victoria Reed, she was the one and only girlfriend of Howard Edward Greenfield. She shared his house, his bed, his dreams. Victoria was like a shot of adrenalin in Howard's veins. He sprang back to life. He returned to work with new energy, new confidence. The former Pork Belly King of Chicago reclaimed his title. He was bold, but not reckless and his instincts were again profitable.

Howard and Victoria were spending a quiet Saturday afternoon in the family room. Both were engrossed in books by Benjamin Sanders. Ben had sent Howard an advanced copy of *The Trial of St. John* with an inscribed note of appreciation for his efforts on behalf of the Sanders family. He also enclosed a signed copy of *Naked Truth*.

Victoria nestled close to Howard on the couch intrigued by the plot of *Naked Truth*. Howard was anxious to finish *The Trial of St. John*.

The Trial of St. John

CHAPTER SIX

THE JUDGE LEANED FORWARD on his desk. "Mr. Prosecutor, we have come to the end of a long journey. Before I render my decision, you may make a final statement, a very brief statement, if you please."

The Prosecutor rose briskly from his chair. His appearance had changed completely just as the status of the Jews had changed completely since the establishment of the State of Israel. He was dressed immaculately in a dark navy suit with a bold Gucci silk tie. His gold cufflinks sparkled and his Italian leather shoes had a bright shine to them. No more soft whispers. He was forceful, assertive, confident.

"Thank you, Your Honor." The Prosecutor turned to face the audience and to face John who was sitting at the defense table.

"It has indeed been a long journey. From the crucifixion of Jesus, to the Crusades, the Inquisition, the Black Death riots, the expulsion from Spain, the pogroms in Poland and Russia and finally the Holocaust.

"It is a miracle that the Jewish people survived 2,000 years of humiliation, torture and murder. But we did survive and now we are back in our home in Israel. Never again will Jews be forced to wear the badge of shame. Never again can Jews be slaughtered like animals while the civilized world does nothing to help them. We walk proud among the peoples of the Earth. Proud of our history, our courage, our faith. Proud of our artists, philosophers, writers, poets. Proud of our entrepreneurs, scientists and statesmen, proud of our generals and farmers. What incredible achievements Jews have given to the world in science, technology, medicine, law and music.

"This trial was called to solve an age-old mystery. Why were the Jews persecuted so brutally century after century after century? Were the Jews guilty of committing crimes wherever they went? They were not. Were the Jews evil people who harmed their neighbors? They were not. The Jews in all the lands they lived were hardworking, honest, religious people. All they wanted was to be left alone. But their Christian neighbors would not leave them alone. They brutalized them, expelled them, tortured them, murdered them. Why? Why were the Jews chosen generation after generation to be victims of unspeakable crimes?

"The reason the Jews were persecuted throughout the centuries is because of the Bible and the lies contained

in the Gospel of John. The first printed Bible was by
Johannes Gutenberg of Germany in 1456. Since that time,
the Bible has been by far the bestselling book in history.
Over 5 billion copies have been sold in 349 languages.
Each copy contains the anti-Semitic messages of the
Gospel of John. You told the world to hate the Jews.
They were the children of the Devil and had killed Jesus
Christ. Is it any wonder that all the hate you spread would
one day culminate in the Holocaust?

"From the time of Gutenberg in 1456 until the end
of the Holocaust in 1945 is 489 years. For all those years,
people around the world read the Bible and believed what
you said about the Jews. Even before Gutenberg printed
the first Bible, thousands of priests used handwritten
Bibles to spread the Holy Word. John you wrote your
Gospel around the end of the 1st century. That means
for 1,300 years before the first Bible was printed priests
were telling Christians that the Jews were an evil people.
For over 1,800 years, priests, ministers and parents were
teaching children to hate Jews. Is it any wonder that
they did?

"The Jews were not like regular human beings, they
were children of the Devil. Why not kill Jews? They were
from the Devil. Why should countries save the Jews from
Hitler? He was killing the Devil's children. Why should
countries open the doors to Jews trying to escape the gas
chambers? Who would want the Devil's children in their
country?

"The Nazi guards at Auschwitz who threw Jewish
babies into the flames did not think of those babies as

humans. They were children of the Devil. How else could someone do such a horrible act?

"The Germans were the most educated people in Europe. How could they participate in the Final Solution? They were also a religious people. They read the Bible. The Catholics and Protestants of Germany believed your words John. The Jews were children of the Devil. Martin Luther also believed your words and wrote how evil the Jews were. Adolf Hitler also believed your words. He called on the Germans to help exterminate the Jews. He called the Jews *Untermenschen*, subhumans and the Germans believed him. Why wouldn't they? For over 1,800 years Christians had been taught that the Jews were different than ordinary people, they were children of the Devil.

"The Bible is sacred to Christians around the world. It is the word of God who inspired those who wrote the Gospels. What is written in the Bible is accepted as the Truth, the "Gospel Truth." John you wrote that the Jews were children of the Devil and millions of Christians believed your words. Jews were not children of God, they were the children of the Devil and that was how they were treated. How else can you explain the Holocaust?

"Hitler and the Nazis were not the only Jew killers. Christians throughout Europe assisted in the roundup of Jews so they could be stuffed into cattle cars and sent to Auschwitz. Why shouldn't they help destroy those children of the Devil you wrote about?

"How else to explain why America refused to accept the Jewish children that Senator Robert Wagner tried to save or why the Jewish passengers of the *St. Louis* were sent back to Germany to perish in the Holocaust?

"Like an ancient witch doctor, you put a curse on the Jews that survives to this day. It is embedded forever in the New Testament. John, you called the Jews children of the Devil and killers of Jesus Christ. That is why the Jews were hated and slaughtered. The Crusaders shouted: 'Kill a Jew and save your soul.' That cry echoed through the centuries.

"John, you did write one statement I agree with. You said: 'Seek ye the truth and the truth will set you free.' That is what this trial is about. We want the truth, the real truth about the crucifixion of Jesus and the anti-Jewish propaganda in the New Testament. The millions of innocent victims of hate cannot be brought back to life. But we can stop that hate from spreading to future generations."

Turning to the Judge, the Prosecutor said: "Your honor, this trial is not about the past. It is about the future. We want a future where Christian children will not be taught to hate Jews. Instead, let them know that the Jesus they worship was a wise and good Jewish rabbi from Galilee. That His message to the world was to love one another.

"Thank you, Your Honor."

Chapter

Thirty-Three

MAX LEVI DECIDED TO give *The Trial of St. John* a gala send off. The party would be at his mansion complete with uniformed butlers, car valets and music from the Chicago Symphony String Quartet. The cold December Saturday night did not keep anyone away. It was the event of the season.

The Chicago area book critics, religion page editors, rabbis, ministers and priests all enjoyed the immense buffet and abundant champagne. Ben had invited Lori O'Connell and her cameraman, Ed Carter, for exclusive TV coverage.

Max couldn't find Sandra Price in the crowd. He decided to check the library. Sandra was standing by the window enchanted by the icy waves dancing in the spotlights. Her slim figure accented by her Vera Wang evening gown. The deep turquoise color was a perfect foil for her delicate features and soft, silver hair. Sandra turned when she heard the door open.

"This room is so magnificent Max. I hope you don't mind I intruded on your private quarters. It was getting a little noisy out there."

"No intrusion at all. You look like you belong here. I suppose you've been told before that you are a very beautiful woman."

"Not often enough. And certainly never by such a distinguished gentleman."

"You know Sandra, you were right."

"Right about what?"

"About my hiding away in this big house. My wife died 8 years ago. I never had a party here until this evening."

"Tell me about your wife. What was she like?"

"What was she like? She was like a sunrise radiating warmth and light and hope. When she died, it left a huge hole in my heart. No amount of money can fill that hole."

"I know Max." Sandra took his hand and kissed it. "I guess we better join the others before the gossips start talking about the two oldsters hiding away in the library."

"Do you feel old Sandra?"

"I feel wonderful and as feisty as ever. It's just that the stupid calendar keeps reminding me that my time is running out. I don't want to go Max. I have so much more to do, to learn, to contribute. I wish time would just stop. I feel like I'm floating on a beautiful river enjoying all the passing scenery and the friendly waves from the people on shore. I love the ride. I'd like it to go on forever.

But I know up ahead or around the next bend or the one after that there is a final waterfall. I can't escape it. No one can and it makes me mad as hell."

"I know just how you feel." Max took Sandra's arm and they rejoined the celebration.

Michael Morris watched as the two senior citizens emerged from the library arm in arm. He smiled to himself. Sandra, you old flirt. Max has really fallen for you. Couldn't happen to two nicer people.

Cindy Cunningham and Sarah Johnson were among the few students invited to the party. They were walking around the Great Room admiring the colorful Monet landscapes that Max had collected. Cindy in her short Kelly green cocktail dress had drawn admiring stares all evening as did Sarah in her black knit evening dress.

"I was surprised you gave up so easily Cindy," Sarah teased her. "I was sure I would lose my $100 bet."

"I was surprised myself," Cindy admitted. "I guess I was wrong about men. They really aren't all alike. I'm glad Professor Sanders turned me down. I would have lost all respect for him."

"I feel bad taking the $100 from you."

"Don't. You won. I lost. That's life."

"I'll give you a chance to win your money back."

"How?"

"Double or nothing. Pick some guy here you think you could seduce and I'll bet you can't."

"For instance who?"

"How about the mysterious man with the glasses and the European accent who met us at the door?"

"He's a strange one isn't he?" Cindy said. "He keeps studying the crowd like he's Secret Service or something."

"Probably is," Sarah agreed. "Well, do you want a second chance to win your money back?"

"No thanks. I decided you and the professor were right. I've stopped playing sex games. I'll try waiting for Mr. Right. He just better come along soon. I don't know how long I can wait."

Adam Vogel watched the two very pretty girls stroll by. He didn't know he had just been spared a delicious encounter with the tall blonde girl in the clinging green dress.

Many guests stopped by the table to see the display of *The Trial of St. John*. The cover was an ornate cross dripping blood on a Torah scroll. On the back cover was a photo of Professor Benjamin Judah Sanders and a short biography.

Nearby, Lori O'Connell was interviewing Father Dominick and Mrs. Bellino. Ben had told Lori to ask the Father about the night he saved Jenny. It would be a good human interest story.

Friends were happy to see that Howard had recovered from his deep depression after the suicide of the girl he had met in France. The girl's cousin from England, a most charming brunette, never left his side as if she feared he might vanish.

A small platform and lectern had been placed in the Great Room in front of the massive stone fireplace. The bright orange flames crackled their warmth. Ben stepped onto the platform and signaled the musicians to stop playing. He rang a large bronze cowbell to get everyone's attention.

"I'd like to thank all of you for coming tonight to help celebrate the publication of *The Trial of St. John*. It has been a long and painful struggle to get this book into print. It would never have happened without the tremendous effort put forth by some truly remarkable people.

"My agent, Michael Morris, refused to take no for an answer. He coaxed Sandra Price out of retirement to start a new company, L'Chaim Publications, so *The Trial of St. John* would have a publisher.

"There were scary problems along the way from kidnapping to blackmail that some of you know about. When it seemed the book would never be published, our host this evening, the amazing Max Levi, came to our rescue. With the assistance of his nephew Howard Edward Greenfield and Adam Vogel the obstacles were removed.

"Finally, and most important, I want to thank my best friend, my wife Michelle and our precious daughter Jenny for their courage in insisting that I publish the book despite possible threats to our family. I am so lucky to have these two incredible women to light up my life.

"To conclude this evening's festivities, I have asked Jenny to read the last few pages of *The Trial of St. John*."

Jenny came to the lectern and looked at all the important people in the room. She spotted Father Dominick and Mrs. Bellino and waved to them. They waved back. Jenny knew she looked pretty. Her Mom had helped brush her long black hair and supervised the light makeup. She was wearing the soft blue dress with the white lace yoke she had worn at her Bat Mitzvah a few months ago. Jenny was so pleased her Dad told her about his plans for this evening. She wasn't nervous. She wanted to do it. She knew she was part of *The Trial of St. John*. She was the reason her Dad had written the book. That horrible night when the four boys had tied her to the cross and stripped her naked was a fading memory, but she had not forgotten. She would never forget. Jenny turned to the page her Dad had marked. Jenny adjusted the microphone and began to read:

The Trial of St. John

CHAPTER SEVEN

THE COURTROOM WAS FILLED to capacity for the final day of the trial. All arguments had been heard, witnesses called from many centuries. Now it was time for the Judge to render his decision. The Judge, wearing his Imperial Roman robe, walked to his throne-like chair in his crisp military manner. The crowd rose as a measure of respect. He motioned them to be seated.

"I spent the last few days reviewing the testimony in this case. The Prosecutor presented in harsh and dramatic fashion the terrible persecution and slaughter of the Jewish people culminating in the Holocaust. The Prosecutor maintains that the seeds of hatred were planted by the Gospel of John. The Jews were blamed for the crucifixion of Jesus and condemned forever as children of the Devil.

"St. John appeared in his own defense. John pointed to the messages of love and brotherhood expressed by Jesus in the New Testament. He called our attention to the hundreds of hospitals and universities founded by various churches and the music, art and cathedrals inspired by the Christian religion."

The Judge looked at the packed courtroom and wondered what impact his ruling would have. Would it make a difference in the world? He hoped so.

"It is a difficult case. I find the charges of anti-Jewish statements in the New Testament to be true. John did write many false and slanderous things about the Jews. On the other hand, we must be careful not to diminish respect for the Bible and the noble teachings of Jesus which are the bedrock of Western Civilization.

"Since I was not present during the hell of the Holocaust, I have sought the judgment of a man who was a witness to that nightmare and a devout Christian. Pope John XXIII convened the Second Vatican Conference which ultimately exonerated the Jews from the crucifixion of Jesus Christ. The Pope died before the Conference had completed its work in 1965, but before he died he composed a special prayer.

"I have accepted the prayer of Pope John XXIII as my final judgment in this case.

"These are the words of Pope John XXIII:

'We now acknowledge that for many, many centuries we were blind to the

Beauty of thy Chosen People and in his face did not recognize the features of our elder brother.

We acknowledge that the mark of Cain is upon our brows. For centuries Abel has lain in blood and tears because we forgot thy love.

Forgive us the curse which we unjustly pronounced upon the Jews.

Forgive us that we crucified Thee for the second time in cursing them.

For we knew not what we did…."'

The Judge leaned forward on his desk. He looked beyond St. John and the Prosecutor to the audience.

"Of course, no one can forgive the Holocaust and no one should ever forget the Holocaust. But to avoid another Holocaust, Christian leaders throughout the world should disavow the tragic lies in the New Testament. The Jews did not kill Jesus. His blood should never, never have been upon them or their children.

"This trial is over. Court adjourned."

The Judge banged his gavel for the final time and walked slowly back through the curtain of history.

Jenny closed the book. There was silence in the room. Then the loud applause began started by Father Dominick.

He was the first to reach the lectern and congratulate Jenny on her fine reading. Ben and Michelle looked on with tears in their eyes as they saw Jenny and Father Dominick embrace one another.

Chapter

Thirty-Four

ON CHRISTMAS EVE, MAX Levi and Adam Vogel sipped coffee together in the library. The lake was quiet, gently lapping on the snow covered rocks below.

"Do you think we should tell them about the *Cocoa Bean*?" Adam asked.

"I was wrong about that," Max admitted. "I thought if we scared Dawn with an attempt on her life Howard could convince her to come back to Chicago with him. That one backfired on us and we almost lost her. I'm glad Howard confided in us that Dawn was alive and was now Victoria Reed."

"Do you think Sheldon Waxman will ever tell Howard it was all a fake and that the Frenchman was hiding below deck while the crew pretended to search for him?"

"Sheldon's a discreet guy," Max replied. "I don't think he would want to embarrass me. For now, let's just leave it alone."

The two old friends, survivors from Hell, watched the restless lake on a beautiful, crisp Christmas Eve. Tomorrow, the whole Christian world would celebrate the birth of Jesus and his message of Peace on Earth, Goodwill towards All. Tonight, these two men were not thinking of Jesus. They were thinking of their families lost in the smoke of Auschwitz.

On the southwest side of Chicago, three men were celebrating Christmas in a different way. West of Harlem Avenue on Roosevelt Road stretched a mile of sacred ground, Waldheim Cemetery, the oldest Jewish cemetery in Chicago. The pioneers of the Jewish community and their descendants were at rest under marble monuments. Hebrew lettering, Jewish stars, loving thoughts were etched into the cold stone. Old photographs adorned the headstones of some of the immigrant Jewish settlers. It was a place of reverence, of respect, of tradition.

The three men were busy working on the red brick walls of Waldheim Cemetery. With bright yellow paint, they put the symbol of hate, the swastika, on the walls of the cemetery. Block after block of yellow swastikas, a Christmas present to the Jewish dead, an insult to the Jewish living.

Over the entrance to the cemetery, they scrawled with yellow paint: "Christ killers." Then they sped away in their car, laughing.

Bibliography

Aarons, Mark and John Loftus, *Unholy Trinity*

Abrahamson, Irving (Editor), *Against Silence: The Voice and Vision of Elie Wiesel*

Allen, Steve, *Religion and Morality*

Arendt, Hannah, *Eichmann in Jerusalem*

Asimov, Isaac, *The Roman Empire*

Augstein, Rudolf, *Jesus Son of Man*

Batey, Richard (Editor), *New Testament Issues*

Beardslee, William A., *Literary Criticism of the New Testament*

Begin, Menachem, *White Nights*

Bentley, Eric, *Rally Cries, Memoirs of Pontius Pilate*

Bickerman, Elias, *From Ezra to the Last of the Maccabees*

Bishop, Jim, *The Day Christ Died*

Bishop, Jim, *The Day Christ Was Born*

Black, Edwin, *The Transfer Agreement*

Bloch, Abraham P., *Day by Day in Jewish History*

Boak, Arthur, *A History of Rome to 565 A.D.*

Bornkamm, G., ~~Jesus of Nazareth~~

Brandon, S.G.F., *The Trial and Death of Jesus*

Bratton, Fred G., *Crimes of Christendom*

Brown, Raymond E., *The Birth of the Messiah*

Brown, Raymond E., *New Testament Essays*

Cahill, Thomas, *The Gifts of the Jews*

Cargas, Harry James, *In Conversation with Elie Wiesel*

Carroll, John, *Constantine's Sword*

Churchill, Winston, *Gathering Storm*

Comay, Joan, *The Diaspora Story*

Cowan, Paul, *An Orphan in History*

Crossan, John Dominic, *Who Killed Jesus?*

Dawidowicz, Lucy, *The Golden Tradition*

Dawidowicz, Lucy, *A Holocaust Reader*

Dawidowicz, Lucy, *The Jewish Presence*

Dawidowicz, Lucy, *The War Against the Jews 1933-1945*

Dayan, Moshe, *Story of My Life*

Dershowitz, Alan M., *Contrary to Public Opinion*

Dickens, Charles, *The Life of our Lord*

Donat, Alexander, *Our Last Days in the Warsaw Ghetto*

Durant, Will, *Caesar and Christ*

Durant, Will, *The Age of Faith*

Edersheim, Alfred, *Sketches of Jewish Social Life*

Flannery, Edward H. (Father), *The Anguish of the Jews*

Fosdick, Harry Emerson, *The Man from Nazareth*

Friday, Nancy, *Men in Love*

Friday, Nancy, *Women on Top*

Friedman, Thomas L., *The Lexus and the Olive Tree*

Gershom, Ezra Ben, *David*

Gervasi, Frank, *The Case for Israel*

Gibran, Kahlil, *Jesus, The Son of Man*

Gilbert, Martin, *The Holocaust*

Girard, Rene', *The Scapegoat*

Glock, Charles Y. and Rodney Stark, *Christian Beliefs and Anti-Semitism*

Goldhagen, Daniel Jonah, *Hitler's Willing Executioners: Ordinary Germans and the Holocaust*

Goldreich, Gloria, *Leah's Journey*

Goodspeed, Edgar J., *A Life of Jesus*

Gordon, Sarah, *Hitler, Germans and the Jewish Question*

Grant, Michael, *Review of the Gospels*

Grant, Robert, *Historical Introduction to the New Testament*

Gray, Martin, *For Those I Loved*

Habe, Hans, *The Mission*

Halevy, Rabbi Yitzchak E., *And Rachel Was His Wife*

Halter, Marek, *The Book of Abraham*

Hamilton, Edith, *The Roman Way*

Hamilton, Edith, *Witness to the Truth*

Harker, Ronald, *Digging up the Bible Lands*

Harmon, Nolan B., *The Interpreter's Bible*

Hertzberg, Arthur, *Jews*

Hilberg, Raul, *The Destruction of the European Jews*

Hitchens, Christopher, *God Is Not Great*

Hoskyns, Sir Edwyn, *The Riddle of the New Testament*

Isaac, Jules, *The Teaching of Contempt, Christian Roots of Anti-Semitism*

Johnson, Paul, *A History of the Jews*

Josephus, Flavius, *Complete Works*

Kahane, Rabbi Meir, *Never Again*

Kamen, Henry, *The Spanish Inquisition*

Kasemann, Ernst, ~~New Testament Questions of Today~~

Kemelman, Harry, *Conversations with Rabbi Small*

Kiefer, Warren, *The Pontius Pilate Papers*

King, Stephen, *Gerald's Game*

Kummel, Werner Georg, *The New Testament*

Lange, Nicholas de, *Atlas of the Jewish World*

Lapide, Pinchas, *Three Popes and the Jews*

Levi, Primo, *Shema, Collected Poems*

Levi, Primo, *The Drowned and the Saved*

Levi, Primo, *Survival in Auschwitz*

Levi, Primo, *If Not Now, When?*

Littell, Franklin, *The Crucifixion of the Jews*

Litvinoff, Barnet, *The Burning Bush, Anti-Semitism and World History*

Lowenthal, Marvin, *The Jews of Germany, A Story of 16 Centuries*

Maccoby, Hyam, *Revolution in Judea*

Marsh, John, *St. John*

Maier, Paul L., *Pontius Pilate*

Michener, James, *The Source*

Moore, Dom Sebastian, *No Exit*

Morse, Arthur D., *While Six Million Died*

Muggeridge, Malcolm, *Jesus Rediscovered*

New Testament, *King James Version*

Nicolson, Harold, *The Meaning of Prestige*

O'Reilly, Bill, *Killing Jesus*

Orenstein, Henry, *I Shall Live*

Oz, Amos, *In the Land of Israel*

Peres, Shiman, *Seven Lives, Israel Founders*

Perrin, Norman, *The New Testament, An Introduction*

234

Perl, William R., *The Holocaust Conspiracy, An International Policy of Genocide*

Perlmutter, Nathan and Ruth Ann, *The Real Anti-Semitism in America*

Poliakov, Leon, *Harvest of Hate*

Potok, Chaim, *The Chosen*

Potok, Chaim, *Wanderings*

Prawer, Joshua, *The World of the Crusaders*

Rand, Ayn, *Atlas Shrugged*

Rubin, Evelyn Pike, *Ghetto Shanghai*

Sachar, Abram Leon, *A History of the Jews*

Samuel, Maurice, *The Professor and the Fossil*

Sandmel, Samuel, *We Jews and You Christians*

Shier, William, *The Third Reich*

Schonfield, Hugh J., *The Jesus Party*

Schonfield, Hugh J., *The Passover Plot*

Schurer, Emil, *The Jewish People*

Schweitzer, Albert, *The Quest of the Historical Jesus*

Silberman, Charles, *A Certain People*

Stone, I.F., *Underground to Palestine*

Stone, Robert, *Damascus Gate*

Syrkin, Marie, *Blessed Is the Match*

Tacitus, Publus Corneluis, *Complete Works of Tacitus*

Tec, Nechama, *When Light Pierced the Darkness*

Trachtenberg, Joshua, *The Devil and the Jews*

Trunk, Isaiah, *Jewish Responses to Nazi Persecution*

Trunk, Isaiah, *Judenrat*

Tuchman, Barbara, *The March of Folly*

Uris, Leon, *Exodus*

Uris, Leon, *Mitla Pass*

~~Vanderlip, D. George, *Christianity According to John*~~

Vegh, Claudine, *I Didn't Say Goodbye*

Vermes, Geza, *Jesus the Jew*

Wallace, Irving, *The Word*

Watts, Harold H., *The Modern Reader's Guide to the Bible*

Wein, Berel, *Triumph of Survival*

Weinreich Max, *Hitler's Professors*

West, Morris L., *The Tower of Babel*

White, Theodore H., *In Search of History*

Wiesel, Elie, *Night*

Wiesel, Elie, *Dawn*

Wiesel, Elie, *Twilight*

Wiesel, Elie, *The Testament*

Wiesel, Elie, *A Jew Today*

Wiesel, Elie, *The Oath*

Wiesenthal, Simon, *Every Day Remembrance Day*

Wingo, Earl L., *A Lawyer Reviews the Illegal Trial of Jesus*

Wilson Edmund, *The Scrolls from the Dead Sea*

Wistrich, Robert S., *Anti-Semitism, The Longest Hatred*

Wyman, David S., *The Abandonment of the Jews*

Yaseen, Leonard C., *The Jesus Connection*

Zeitlin, Solomon, *Who Crucified Jesus?*

Printed in the United States
By Bookmasters